As Lord Dornfor... waistcoat Miran... from the bed. *"You are welcome to go to your bed, my lord. I will come later."*

He walked slowly and unsteadily across the room. *" 'Tis late already, boy, so do not argue with me."*

When he was close enough to Miranda he caught hold of her by both arms and began to propel her across the room. Bewildered and fearful she began to struggle but it was unequal despite his fuddled condition.

"Please unhand me, my lord," she pleaded.

Panic-stricken, she wrenched herself away from his grip and a most terrible thing happened; a rending sound cut the air as the shirt tore open to reveal the petticoat bodice beneath.

Miranda cried out in fright, clasping her arms about her, and the marquis's eyes opened wide in disbelief. He blinked twice and then gasped, *"The devil take it; 'tis a woman!"*

Miranda's Folly

RACHELLE EDWARDS

FAWCETT CREST • NEW YORK

MIRANDA'S FOLLY

THIS BOOK CONTAINS THE COMPLETE TEXT
OF THE ORIGINAL HARDCOVER EDITION.

Published by Fawcett Crest Books, a unit of CBS Publi-
cations, the Consumer Publishing Division of CBS Inc.,
by arrangement with Robert Hale Limited.

ISBN: 0-449-23992-6

Selection of the Doubleday Romance Library

Printed in the United States of America

10   9   8   7   6   5   4   3   2   1

Love is the wisdom of the fool and the folly of the wise.

Dr. Samuel Johnson

Chapter One

Night had long since fallen and yet activity continued at the "Bell Inn". In her first floor bedchamber Miranda could hear the almost constant rattle of carriage wheels in the yard outside, the clip-clop of hooves accompanied by the shouts of the postboys and ostlers. She listened in fascination to the unfamiliar sounds and wondered if they would ever stop long enough to allow her to sleep. Someone shouted—a voice she had not heard before—the sound followed by the thump of baggage being unloaded onto the cobbles.

From within the building she could hear the voices of revellers raised in bawdy song and the frequent use of words by the ostlers which caused her to blush. Inside of her, fear mingled with excitement, for soon she would be in London. Soon she would see Myles again . . . and Cornelius too. The thought sustained her as she glanced around the shabby bedchamber,

the uninviting bed with its none too clean
linen.

She wished Jed, the groom, could have accompanied her all the way to London, but that
was out of the question. He had come as far as
he could and stayed away from the house as
long as he dared. Untying her purse she quickly counted the coins it contained. There was
more than enough to see her to London despite
the exhorbitant price she had been obliged to
pay for this modest room and the meal of over-
cooked beef and watery cabbage. Of course, it
was always possible a highwayman might stop
the coach tomorrow, and as an afterthought
Miranda put half the coins in her cloakbag and
replaced the purse to her pocket.

It was growing late, the candle was burning
low, but even if it was quiet enough for sleep
the excitement within her prevented it. Nor
did she relish removing her clothes and lying
between those sheets in an unfamiliar bed.
Fastidious as ever, she shied away from the
thought, longing for the comfort of the laven-
der-scented and well-aired linen she was accustomed to at home.

After a few moments she crossed to the window and pulled back the curtains gingerly. In
the courtyard there stood a chaise—a private
one—with mud splashes marring the elegant
green coachwork. Above it the inn sign creaked
rhythmically in the wind which rattled at the
casements.

Miranda let the curtain fall and walked back to the washstand, peering at her reflection in the mirror. What she saw made her smile slightly. The copper-coloured curls, so familiar to all who knew her, were now powdered to an indiscriminate brown and tied back with a black ribbon, her womanly figure disguised beneath a man's brocade coat and breeches. It was a good disguise, she reflected, and no one could guess she was not what she appeared to be.

In the dim light she noticed for the first time that the lace on the shirt was torn and realised this was why Myles had discarded it. The coat, she also suspected, was of an outmoded style, no longer suited to a man-about-town. She had heard that gentlemen of mode were beginning to sport less ostentatious fashions, but not so with the ladies who, according to the fashion-plates she studied, were plumed and as extravagantly gowned as ever. Miranda looked forward to seeing the fashionable ladies of London of whom she had heard and dreamed of so much.

The candle flickered in a draught and drawing a sigh of resignation Miranda took off the coat and draped it over the back of a chair. She walked to the bed and holding up the candle with one hand she pulled back the covers gingerly with the other, inspecting the bedding as minutely as she could in so sparse a light.

After a few moments she straightened up

and placed the candle on a side table. She poured a little water into the washbowl and splashed it over her face. As she dried herself on the coarse towel provided Miranda realised that she need go no farther. There was still time to return home and no one would be the wiser to her escapade. Just at that moment in the strange and shabby room it was a temptation, and then resolutely she pushed the idea away. The plan had been formulating in her mind for weeks; she just had to go on now or regret the lost opportunity for the rest of her life.

She threw down the towel and went back to the bed, slowly sinking down on to the mattress. It felt hard but she ignored the discomfort. After all it was only to be for one night. In two days she would be in London and hopefully enjoying the comforts to which she was accustomed. With some difficulty she pulled off the ill-fitting boots and then, removing the linen neckcloth, began to unfasten the shirt.

Just as she began her hands froze at what appeared to be a commotion on the stairs. Sound seemed to travel easily because of the bareness of the walls and floors of the inn and every noise was a loud one. Involuntarily her heart began to beat noisily and she hurried across to the door to listen. She had supposed no one would think to pursue her but suddenly she was not so sure. Pursuit was all too possible if Papa began to suspect she was not where she ought to be.

Heavy feet were treading the stairs and Miranda listened with held breath as they approached her chamber. The footsteps grated on the floorboards outside the door and Miranda was suddenly assailed by panic. She glanced across at the window, knowing even then that escape was useless and indeed unnecessary. If Papa had sent to fetch her back she had no alternative but to go.

Before she had a chance to react further there came a ferocious thumping on the door which made her start.

"Master! Open up there, master!"

Miranda recognised the voice of the landlord, which afforded her no reassurance. She backed towards the bed and stood there with her back rigidly against the post, her heart beating so loud she feared it might burst.

"Master! Open up, I say!"

"Who . . . who is there?" she asked in a tremulous voice.

"A weary traveller to share the room, master."

Miranda knew that it was often necessary for travellers to share accommodation but after making anxious enquiries she had been assured this would not be necessary.

After waiting a moment she moved towards the door again and hesitated once more before lifting the latch and opening the door a fraction. Out in the corridor she could see the corpulent bulk of the landlord who was holding up a candle, a maid-servant carrying a tray with a glass and bottle set upon it, and a postboy stooping under the weight of a valise. Miranda looked at them all fearfully and then to a man in the shadows behind them; he appeared to be leaning nonchalantly against the opposite wall, but she could not see him clearly at all.

Returning her attention to the landlord she said, "What is the meaning of this intrusion? I have paid for the sole use of this room and was just about to retire when you disturbed me."

"There's nought I can do about it, lad. 'is Lordship 'ere 'as 'ad an unfortunate encounter and cannot continue 'is journey. 'e needs a room for the night and none other than this one is available."

"There must be another," she complained. "This inn is a large one."

"Aye, but the stage goes on the morrow. We be full up tonight."

"It's impossible for him to come in here."

The landlord did not trouble to reply; he pushed open the door almost knocking Miranda to the floor as he did so. She recovered her balance and scampered into the centre of the room, panic rising fast as the maidservant came in and put the tray down, followed by the postboy with the valise.

"This way, your lordship," invited the landlord in silky tones.

"Get out!" Miranda ordered in a frightened voice as the maidservant busied herself restoring the dying fire. "I insist that you all leave this room immediately."

"Don't get into a pucker, lad," the landlord said in a low voice, "This 'ere's the Quality."

Miranda was in no way impressed. "There must be another room," she said in desperation.

"Wish I 'ad a better one," he answered ruefully as the new occupant straightened up and sauntered, not quite steadily, into the room.

Miranda transferred her attention to this object of her fear and immediately gained an impression of great height. The room had grown a little lighter with the introduction of another candle which the landlord had put down near the tray. Broad-shouldered and enveloped in a many-caped driving coat of dark broadcloth this man looked very alarming indeed. He seemed totally unaware of Miranda's presence as his dark gaze frowningly took in every aspect of this room.

"I've paid for this room," Miranda hissed under her breath.

"Yer'll get yer money back, lad, 'ave no fear o' that."

"If you insist this person use this room *I* want to be transferred to another."

The landlord gave her an exasperated look. "Ain't got another, 'aven't I been telling yer that?"

The landlord's eyes returned to the new guest's face and they seemed to be alight with excitement. As the newcomer put one hand to his purse and drew out some coins which he tossed to the maid and the postboy, Miranda realised why and was angered anew.

The landlord sidled up to him, saying, "This 'ere's the best room in the inn, m'lord. I 'ope it'll do."

The newcomer looked down at the landlord in a disdainful way. "It will have to do," he answered, speaking for the first time, "seeing there is no alternative. I trust the bed linen is clean and the brandy undiluted."

"Oh yes, m'lord. Never do that would the landlord of the 'Bell'."

The man laughed harshly and the chink of coins told Miranda that the landlord had been well rewarded. As the newcomer drew off his coat the landlord came back towards Miranda on his way out of the room and his manner had changed from one of obsequiousness to belligerence.

"Now see 'ere, m'lad, don't you go and be cheeky to his lordship, and don't go keepin' 'im awake."

"He can't stay . . .", she began to protest, but the landlord had gone, closing the door behind him.

Quaking with fear and anger Miranda turned on the newcomer now. "Who do you think you are, forcing your way in here?"

The man turned to glance at her for the first time before continuing to pour a glass of brandy. "Allow me to introduce myself since the landlord was remiss in doing so; James Devilliars, Seventh Marquis of Dornford at your service. The landlord is an uncouth devil."

Miranda found that her breath was coming in short frightened gasps and she put her hand to her breast in an effort to still its heaving.

"It is inexcusable," she gasped. "I have paid for the sole use of this bedchamber."

In answer Lord Dornford placed a few coins on the table and then to her further chagrin tossed his coat over a chair and lowered himself into another, facing her at last.

"I was about to retire . . .", she insisted.

He waved one hand in the air. "Please don't let me stop you, boy." His manner momentarily softened. "You've nought to fear from me, and the bed is big enough for both."

She drew in an indignant breath, looking fearfully at the bed but for quite a different reason than previously.

"Just because you're Quality doesn't give you the right to do just as you please."

He laughed again as he drained his glass. "It surely must give me some advantage." He poured out more brandy and then looked at Miranda again. "I cannot for the life of me understand the pucker you're in. I don't like this God-forsaken place, this inferior hostelry, any more than you, lad, but for tonight we both

must needs make the best of it. I told the landlord there was no need to dispossess you of this
room. . . ."

"You!" she cried out. "I was here first!"

The marquis seemed unaware of her anger
as he held his filled glass up to the light to in-
spect the quality of the brandy. That seemed
to be of the utmost importance to him.

"Come," he coaxed a moment later, "bring
me your glass and we shall drink a toast
together."

Miranda mutely shook her head. Should she
go down to the coffee room and spend the night
there? she wondered, but immediately disregarded the idea. The coffee room would be a far
more perilous place, filled with drunks unable
or unwilling to travel further. She had considered so many eventualities, but the chance of
something like this happening had never occurred to her.

The marquis's eyes narrowed and he sat forward in the chair. "How old are you, boy?"

She thought quickly and then, drawing in a
short breath, answered, "I am sixteen."

"And barely that by the looks of you. Is this
the first time you've been away from home
alone?"

Miranda nodded and he smiled knowingly.
"How well I know that feeling. I remember it
well although I was younger than you and had
three servants to serve me on my first long
journey from home."

He got to his feet which caused her to shrink away from him fearfully. His size seemed to fill the room, making it appear smaller than before. She watched his every movement as he prowled around the room and then sighed with relief when he appeared to find what he was looking for near the wash stand—a drinking glass. He filled it with brandy and held it out to her. When she made no move to take it he laughed again, something which alarmed her anew. His laughter had such a wild sound to it.

"You hope to be a man one day, don't you?" he taunted.

"Yes." It was barely a whisper.

"Then take this glass and drink a toast with me."

Hesitantly she came forward to take it from him, realising that this was not the first bottle of brandy he had consumed since arriving at the inn. Nevertheless, he appeared to be holding his liquor well.

The marquis sat down again, this time stretching his legs out in front of him to be warmed by the fire. He raised his glass slowly. "To Mad Earle. May he rot in Hell where he belongs."

He downed the glassful in one gulp as Miranda said, still clutching hers, "Mad who?"

"The beggar of a highwayman who tried to rob me this evening. But for him I would have been at a far superior hostelry twenty miles hence, enjoying its comfort and attended by my own valet."

Miranda was for the moment diverted from the problems of her predicament and wide-eyed asked, "You were attacked by a highwayman?"

"He tried," the marquis amended as he refilled his glass. The bottle, she noted, was almost empty. "He was not to know he tried to rob the wrong man. I knocked the pistol from his cowardly fingers and boxed him well about the ears." He patted his purse and smiled. "Every penny piece is intact."

He peered than at the diamond ring which adorned his little finger. The enormous gem leaped with fire as it caught the light. "Sent him running like a whipped cur," he mused. "Drink up, lad! The stuff's well-watered and can't harm even a babe like you. It'll make a man of you, you'll see!"

Miranda could not help but laugh at this, albeit nervously. Attempting to emulate his lordship she drank the brandy down in the same way, as much as she could manage in one gulp. The resultant coughing and spluttering as the brandy burned her throat sent the marquis into transports of fuddled laughter.

"That is," he gasped, "an important aspect of your education attended to."

Furious at his mockery Miranda flung the empty glass into a corner where it shattered into many pieces, fuelling Lord Dornford's laughter. As the paroxyms of coughing and his laughter died down the marquis said, "You have the advantage of me, boy. What's your name?"

After a moment's hesitation she sank down onto the edge of the bed. Her legs felt weak but that dreadful fire water had in some way removed the awful fear she had been feeling. She had always been considered quick-witted and she realised that if she did keep her wits about her the night would pass without incident and in the morning she could be aboard the London stagecoach without anyone being the wiser about her true identity. The marquis was already well on his way to being drunk.

"Crawley, sir. Master Crawley's the name."

"Well, Master Crawley, do you think you could act the part of a valet and pull m'boots?"

It was a great temptation to refuse but she decided against such a course. Nothing must be allowed to raise his suspicions about her. A little fearfully she approached and after a moment's hesitation she pulled at one mud-splattered hessian. It didn't move.

Nursing his glass, the marquis regarded her with amusement. "You'll have to pull harder than that, Master Crawley."

Biting her lip in an attempt to contain the anger which was now fast rising inside her, she pulled again. This time the boot did come off, but Miranda fell on her back too. The marquis roared with laughter but she was furious again and as she scrambled to her feet she threw down the boot which had remained clutched in her arms.

"You're despicable!" she cried, willing herself not to cry and therefore give herself away.

The marquis seemed untroubled by the accusation as he poured out more brandy. "And you are an ill-mannered brat."

"I feel sorry for Mad Earle. Wretched as he is he must be a far better kind of creature than you and I wish he'd beaten you. It would have taught you a lesson."

He looked at her again and this time there was a cold expression in his eyes which suddenly chilled her. "You are looking to have your ears boxed, boy, and I would need little more encouragement to do it. Now be a good fellow and pull my other boot."

Miranda folded her arms resolutely in front of her. "No, I will not."

Lord Dornford smiled, "I can, even now, ask the landlord to remove you from my room."

Miranda stamped her foot with impotent rage and as he patiently waited for her to remove his boot she knew she really had no choice. Not for the first time in her life did she wish she were really a man so she could deal with him as he deserved. Men, she had observed on so many occasions received every advantage in life whereas females were so often sadly left in want.

She managed to remove the boot, this time

retaining her dignity and then she retreated to the far side of the room and sat down on the very edge of the bed. She watched with scarce-concealed hatred as he drained the last drop from the bottle.

"Do you live hereabouts?" he asked and she was amazed that his speech remained not the slightest bit slurred.

Her thoughts milled furiously in her brain and when he looked at her questioningly she answered in a muted voice, "I come from a little place called Kesselwell, some miles from here."

"A village, eh? I might have guessed you were a rustic. And where, may I ask, are you bound?"

"London."

One dark eyebrow went up a fraction. "London indeed. What the devil takes a callow youth like you to London?"

"Not . . . not London itself, my lord," she added as an afterthought, "Paddington, which I believe is some way out of the town itself. That is my ultimate destination."

"I know it. A village of no particular distinction. What business have you there?"

Miranda bit her lip, aware that he was watching her and awaiting an answer.

"I am going to see my . . . er . . . godmother," she answered at last. "She . . . she is mortally ill and has asked for a sight of me before she dies."

"A tale to touch the heart," he said dryly. "No doubt the consideration of a share in the poor woman's estate did not enter into your mind before you set out to rush to her bedside."

Miranda recoiled from such obvious sarcasm. "Certainly not! That is a dreadful thing to say. You know nothing of the matter."

He laughed harshly. "You are quite correct and I stand chastised, but if you hope to journey from here on the London stage you may yet reach the afterworld before her."

"You are a cynic, sir."

He sat up a little straighter. "And you speak well for a rustic. Why are you travelling alone?"

"My parents are unable to accompany me, sir. My father is a . . . mercer in the village where we live and unable to leave the shop at this time, and I could not delay lest it be too late to comfort her."

"Is that also true of your mother?"

"You ask a great many questions," she said resentfully.

"It is a long night."

"I have several younger brothers and sisters and she could not leave them," Miranda answered resignedly. "My parents deemed me old enough to journey on my own."

"And so you are, except . . . well . . . you have a certain naivite unusual in youths of sixteen. No doubt your mama has coddled you unduly. It is a vice prevalent in most mothers I notice."

"But not yours," she could not help but counter.

He sighed and regarded his empty glass. "Alas, mine is long dead, Master Crawley. You do not know how fortunate you are."

She could find nothing to say and as he stared into the fire they lapsed into a silence she found suddenly unwelcome. With the introduction of an extra candle and the remaking of the fire, the room was considerably lighter than before. Looking at him properly now Miranda realised he had not escaped entirely without cost during his encounter with Mad Earle. The greatcoat which he'd thrown over a chair was splattered with mud as were his breeches. His blue velvet coat was torn at the sleeve and so was his shirt and a bruise was beginning to show lividly on his cheek, just below the eye.

"You, I suspect, Lord Dornford, are far from home," she ventured after a while.

It was, as he had pointed out, going to be a long night, much longer than she had anticipated, and it must needs be got through as comfortably as was possible in the circumstances.

"Ah, so you too have become curious?"

Her cheeks grew red. "Conversation will help the time pass the quicker."

"And for a growing lad you show yourself ill-disposed towards sleep."

"Your coming disturbed me, and I no longer feel like sleeping."

He drew out a gold snuff box and painstakingly took a pinch before answering in an indolent voice, "I've been negotiating the purchase of a parcel of prime farmland not too far distant from here. My land steward who accompanied me returned home yesterday, but my host pressed me to remain a further night, mainly I suspect because he wished to acquaint me further with the charms of his exceedingly plain sister." He wagged his finger at her. "Be warned, Master Crawley, the wiles of desperate women. They will have you if they can."

"You are not wed?"

"Not I," he answered proudly.

Rather awkwardly he got to his feet which made her start and feel apprehensive once more. He swayed unsteadily but held on to the table.

"The brandy was more potent than I supposed," he murmured to himself. "Perchance that landlord did not lie."

Miranda automatically got up too and moved away from the bed. Come what may she would not—could not—share a bed with this most dissolute of men. The thought caused her to shiver uncontrollably.

After a few moments he managed to remove

his coat and unfasten the striped-brocade waistcoat beneath it. She watched with bated breath as he removed his time-piece from his pocket and stared as it. It soon became obvious the brandy had at last taken its toll of him, for he was having some difficulty in focusing properly.

"The hour is late," he said at last. " 'Tis long past time for bed. For you too, young man, if you wish to catch the stage tomorrow. Come, let us both retire. Your doting mama will expect no less of you."

As he struggled to remove his waistcoat Miranda moved further away from the bed. "You are welcome to go to your bed, my lord. I will come later."

He walked slowly and unsteadily across the room. " 'Tis late already, boy, so do not argue with me."

When he was close enough to Miranda he caught hold of her by both arms and began to propel her across the room. Bewildered and fearful she began to struggle but it was unequal despite his fuddled condition.

"Please unhand me, my lord," she pleaded.

He merely laughed. "You blush and stammer like a maiden. I do believe you're bashful!"

He had managed to pull her as far as the bed at which point she howled with anguish and made one last bid to free herself from his grip. She wrenched herself away from him, which caused him to lose his balance and stumble backwards onto the bed, dragging her with him. He lay there roaring with laughter which caused someone in the adjoining chamber to knock on the wall and shout some abuse Miranda could not quite hear. The marquis did not heed it and she could feel his heart beating beneath her and the faint smell of eau de cologne assailed her senses. Her head began to reel but making the most of this opportunity she began to drag herself away from him once more.

"This is unwarranted," she protested. "You will regret this uncouth behaviour come the morning. You are so bosky you do not know what you're about."

As she stood up, hurriedly straightening the shirt, he sat up too, saying, "I am never too bosky to know what I am about."

As she backed away he reached out to catch hold of her again but he only managed to grasp the front of the shirt. Panic-stricken she wrenched herself away from his grip and a most terrible thing happened; a rending sound cut the air as the shirt tore open to reveal the petticoat bodice beneath.

Miranda cried out in fright, clasping her arms about her, and the marquis's eyes opened wide in disbelief. He blinked twice and then gasped, "The devil take it; 'tis a woman!"

He struggled to get to his feet as she backed away, really knowing what fear was now. He reached out to her with one hand, failed to catch hold of her and then, swaying on his feet, he keeled over onto the bed and lay still. Miranda stood transfixed, clutching the remnants of the shirt about her. Suddenly the only sound to be heard was the rasping of her own uneven breathing.

After a few moments, during which the marquis remained completely motionless, she inched towards him, still hugging her arms around her body. As she approached he emitted a loud snore and she drew back only to realise he had fallen into a drunken stupor and wasn't likely to trouble her again.

Feeling almost faint with relief, she sank down on to the edge of the bed to collect her composure. Her mind was numb as she tried to think what to do, and tears squeezed involuntarily from beneath her lids. Some minutes passed and the silence became oppressive. One candle flickered feebly and then died. As Miranda watched it dazedly she realised she had best get out of there as quickly as she was able.

She brushed away her tears and hurried to where her cloakbag had been left on the floor, and quickly found the spare shirt she had fortunately put into it. Glancing fearfully behind her at the marquis who was now sleeping heavily she stripped off what was left of the shirt and put on the fresh one. Over it she put the coat on and gripping her cloakbag and the hat she had earlier disregarded she hurried towards the door.

Only when she had reached it did she realise there was nowhere for her to go. Even now she had no desire to return home and she certainly could not leave the inn if she still intended to board the coach which left for London from here at six o'clock in the morning. Lord Dornford would sleep well beyond that hour.

Miranda put down the bag and turned back into the room. She tip-toed to the bed and gazed down at the marquis. The bruise was now a brilliant purple, she noticed. On the other cheek she saw for the first time what might have been a duelling scar. His hair was very dark, but dishevelled now and escaping the ribbon which held it back. The eyelashes which fanned out on his cheeks were dark too and of a length any female might envy. There was a faint stubble appearing on his chin and she guessed that with his colouring he must needs shave often to preserve an immaculate appearance. His dishevelled appearance on this occasion, she sensed, would not be habitual.

All in all, she mused, in the normal way he would be a fine-looking man. Only a vile nature marred what might have been an admirable member of the aristocracy.

Miranda lifted his legs onto the bed and pulled the coverlet up to his chin, starting with fear as he clutched at her hand in his sleep. Ever so carefully she disengaged it and held her breath momentarily as he stirred and then settled again. She tip-toed across the room and found his time-piece lying on the table where he had left it. There was only a few hours left before the stage was due to leave. She would not sleep now.

Careful to make no noise she drew a chair towards the fire and lowered herself into it, covered by the marquis's greatcoat. Without taking her eyes from his inert form Miranda settled down to her vigil.

Chapter Two

The stagecoach shook and bumped over every rut and hole in the road, and there were many of them. Squeezed between a fat lady nursing a fretsome child and a parson who had scarce lifted his eyes from his bible, Miranda felt the journey would never end. Belatedly she recalled the Marquis of Dornford's warning on the perils of coach travelling and reflected that he had exaggerated little.

A schoolboy in the far corner kept grinning at her and making weird faces to which she had at first responded in a like manner, but now all she was aware of was the aching of every bone in her body. It was hours since the last stop and it was now growing dark—and cold. She might have felt less travel-weary had she been able to sleep the night before, but her eyes had never closed. On the night previous to that she had found sleep difficult to come by too, because of the excitement of anticipation.

Embarking on this journey Miranda had not

really considered how uncomfortable it would be. Aware of the peril in any well-bred young lady journeying alone she had decided to travel as a boy, but in view of what had occurred last night that had proved hardly less perilous.

The memory of the previous evening still caused her to shudder from time to time with shame and embarrassment, and it had been with great relief she had boarded the stagecoach with no sign of the marquis abroad. With luck he would not even remember what had ensued that night when he awoke from his stupor. It was one consolation and she wished she too had been too drunk to remember.

She tried to take her mind off her discomfort by peering out of the window at the darkening landscape, but there was precious little of interest to be seen at this time of the year, the time when the countryside slumbered and yet London came into its own. With every jolt of the stagecoach she was a little bit nearer to her goal.

In the other corner facing her sat a timid-looking woman whom Miranda placed as a governess or some other senior servant on her way to a new position. Deep within her she felt a stirring of pity and as she caught the woman's eye smiled slightly.

"I hear a notorious highwayman frequents this road," she said in a whisper, as if afraid the very mention of it would cause the fiend to appear.

"It's all the same if he does hold up the stage," said the schoolboy. "I've little enough to surrender."

The thin woman seemed to have paled and huddled deeper into the squabs. Miranda could not help but chuckle and felt bound to answer, "I have a notion that creature will not be fit to haunt the highway for some time to come."

No one questioned her knowledge. As a mere youth her opinion would not be valued, but she had at least comforted the nervous lady who then ventured, "It grows dark so rapidly. We should be nearing our stop for dinner soon."

"I hope so," muttered the schoolboy. "I'm hungry enough to eat a horse."

"You might have to if the coach breaks an axle or wheel on these roads," answered the bluff-looking man who was sandwiched between them.

The woman looked horrified. "Do you really think so?"

"I doubt it," Miranda felt bound to say in a matter-of-fact tone. "I have just seen the lights of an inn across that field. It cannot be more than a mile or two down the road."

The woman looked relieved and lapsed back into a more customary silence, but the bluff-looking man had found his tongue.

"It's to be hoped the food and lodging's a bit better than the 'Bell'. Spent the night there, I did," he told his captive audience. "Terrible place, but they always are, so I'm told. I never had a moment's sleep last night. Such a commotion in the room next to mine. Some gent had his lightskirt in there. Fighting and carrying on all the while, but I must say it is one way of passing a night in a disagreeable inn. Could have done with a bit more pleasant company myself," he added, glaring meaningfully at the parson.

The thin woman gasped and Miranda felt her cheeks flooding with colour and looked away quickly. The parson, who at last lifted his head from his bible, fixed the talker with a steely stare.

"Sir, I would ask that you moderate your language in the company of ladies."

The bluff-looking man had no time to reply for at that moment the coach slowed its pace drastically and turned a corner. Miranda was thrown sideways onto the parson and the fat woman onto her. The thin woman screamed but a few moments later it became clear, as the coach drew into an inn courtyard, that none of them was hurt. Miranda sat up and straightened her coat, the fat lady was trying to pacify her child and the thin lady in the opposite corner was straightening her bonnet.

As the coach trundled to a halt Miranda had never been more glad of a respite. Whatever fare and rest the inn afforded would be welcome on this night. She would not, it was certain, remain awake, however hard the bed, if indeed such a thing was available to her.

All the passengers including those outside in the basket tottered into the inn which immediately afforded welcome warmth. A postboy just inside the dinner room accosted the schoolboy who said something rude, shook of the importuning hand and rushed over to the refectory table where supper was laid out. If the mutton was tough and the vegetables tasteless it would be of no matter to Miranda, so hungry and tired. Her own bed and the comforts of home seemed an age away.

As she followed the schoolboy and the others who were busy seating themselves around the table the postboy put one hand on her arm, looking at her anxiously.

"Master Crawley?"

"Yes?" Miranda answered in some surprise.

"Come this way, sir. A private parlour is awaiting you."

She laughed and stood her ground. "There must be some mistake. I have not bespoken a private parlour."

"There is no mistake, master. Please follow me."

A little bemusedly she did follow him across the hall where he flung open the door to a smaller room.

"Master Crawley, my lord."

"Ah, do come in, Master Crawley. I have

been waiting for you for an age. The stage arrived much later than expected."

Miranda stopped still in the doorway, her legs turning to water and she gripped hold of the wall to steady herself. Inside the parlour a table was laid with fare more sumptuous than in the dining room, and on a white cloth stood chafing dishes filled with veal cutlets, sliced lamb, pigeon pie, syllabub and apple pie. In the hearth a fire blazed, and in front of the fire, one foot resting on the hearth rail, one arm on the mantel, stood none other than the Marquis of Dornford.

She thought she must be dreaming, or rather having a nightmare. It was impossible for him to be here. She had left him still deep in the stupor, and yet here he undoubtedly was, not only awake but alert too and looking as if he'd been there for some time.

His hair was glossy and in place now, his coat of last evening had been disregarded for one of dark blue broadcloth, the torn shirt replaced by one of the finest cambric and lace, his breeches were without a trace of mud and his boots polished so highly she could almost see her reflection in them. Only the bruise on his cheek and the duelling scar remained the same, which proved beyond doubt it was he, and she was not dreaming after all.

As she stared at him in disbelief for some few moments he gazed back at her, his expression one of amusement. "Do come in, Master

Crawley," he said in a voice heavy with irony.
"The open door is causing a draught and the
fire is smoking."

Miranda took a few steps forward and the
postboy slammed the door shut, causing her to
start uneasily.

"Don't be afraid," he said. "I mean you no
harm. Come and sit down. Your bones must
ache after all these hours in the coach."

She put one hand to her head. "How . . .
how. . . .?"

He smiled blandly. "How did I get here before you?" he kindly interpolated.

He moved away from the fire and took the
snuff box from his pocket. After he had flicked
open the lid and taken a pinch he returned his
attention to Miranda, putting the snuff box
away again.

"It was all too easy. My team is, I say without fear of contradiction, one of the best—no,
the best—in the land. It was no hardship over-
taking so cumbersome an object as the London
stage." He glanced at his time-piece. "At about
noon today. The old nags harnessed to the
stage are no match for my chestnuts."

"But even so, you were still in a stupor when
I left this morning. How can you have recovered so easily?"

"My dear, it would take more than two
bottles of cheap brandy to lay me low. Fortunately my valet at last caught up with me and
rendered me a little more presentable to the

world. Of course, it did mean I had to hurry my breakfast, for which I cannot thank you."

He sauntered across to the table and waved one hand in the air. "What will you eat? I'll wager you are half-starved by now." He glanced at her slyly and then turned away again. "The pigeon pie is delicious, or perhaps you would prefer some minced turkey?"

Miranda needed no reminder of her hunger but answered, "Supper is awaiting me in the dining room."

"You cannot wish to join that crush. You will fare much better in here." With no further ado he began to pile the plate with something from each dish and when he presented it to her, hunger overcame both pride and apprehension.

Still feeling somewhat bemused she sat down in a chair near to the fire and began to consume every morsel he had put out for her. When she was about halfway through the meal she realised he was sitting on a chair facing her, a bottle and a glass at his side, and he was studying her carefully through heavy-lidded eyes.

"Are you not going to eat too?" she asked hesitantly, feeling suddenly conscious of her zeal.

"I have already eaten. Please continue."

Miranda ate slowly now, knowing that when she had finished the time of reckoning would be near. He had pursued her with a particular purpose in mind. What that purpose could be she deliberately refused to consider. All she could do was delay the reckoning for as long as possible.

At last she could forestall him no longer. He sat back at ease in his chair, surveying her over the rim of his glass as she put down the plate.

"Now, madam," he said, "you may tell me why you are travelling the King's highway masquerading as a boy."

In a less than even voice she answered, "It is no concern of yours, my lord, how I wish to travel."

"I am making it my concern. Make no mistake, you do not leave this room until I have heard the truth of the matter."

As she straightened up she could see that his face wore an uncompromising look and she was quite certain he meant what he said.

"And," he added, "I want none of that tarra-diddle about a dying god-mother in Paddington. My heart is not so easily wrung, miss."

"I am persuaded, Lord Dornford, that you do not have one."

His lips curled into an ironic smile. "That question has often been the subject of debate and no doubt if the matter could be proved one way or the other wagers would be put upon it."

Miranda got to her feet slowly. "I thank you for the excellent supper, but I regret I must join my fellow travellers with no more delay."

She turned to go and continuing to sip his

brandy he told her, "Be assured, miss, you will not be allowed to leave until I am satisfied I have your explanation."

She turned on her heel. "What can it matter to you?"

He shrugged. "It is not every day I come upon a female dressed as a boy, and I am curious."

Her eyes flashed fire as she strove to contain her anger. "Then you will have to remain curious. You cannot keep me here against my will. The inn is crowded and I can easily shout for help."

"In that event more than I will be aware you are a woman. You do give yourself away in many small ways, you know. I am convinced had I not been slightly bosky last night you would not have fooled me above a few minutes."

"You flatter yourself, my lord."

He paused to pour more brandy for himself and as Miranda reached the door he went on, "It really will do you no good to create confusion; I have already told the landlord I am here to return my runaway brother to his school."

Miranda was speechless for a moment and then she cried, "You are vile!"

"Yes," he answered imperturbably, "so I am often told. I am beginning to believe it must be true."

Knowing he had the best of her she sank down into the chair again. Seeing he knew her to be a woman she decided to act like one and accordingly burst into a torrent of noisy tears which because of the circumstances was particularly easy to achieve.

He allowed her to weep for a short while and then he stood up and came towards her. "That is much better, Miss. . . .?"

"Crawley," she gulped, and then as she looked up into his face she added, "It really is. There is no point in my telling you anything if you refuse to believe everything I say."

He handed her a lace-edged handkerchief and she began to mop up her tears. He turned his back on her and walked away, much to her relief. His presence near to her was far more disconcerting than when he was far away, discomforting as that was. She wished him a thousand miles away.

"You are not, I hope, Miss *William* or Miss *Thomas* Crawley. I hope you will not seek to assure me of *that*."

She couldn't help but laugh. "Miranda. My name is Miranda Crawley."

He turned sharply on his heel, stared at her until she had to look away in confusion, and then conceded, "Very well, Miss Miranda Crawley it is." He leaned back against the table and folded his arms in front of him. "Now we have established your name you may tell me the rest of it, miss, and watch what you say. My mind is perfectly clear today and I've no mind to listen to a farrago of lies."

"There would be no point now," she said in a piteous voice.

"Indeed not."

She began to pull at the handkerchief which was now damp and sadly crumpled. "It is a long and wearisome tale," she warned. "You will not find it as interesting as you suppose."

"I do not seek interest, only a measure of enlightenment. I have all the time in the world at my disposal," he added blandly. "Tell me where you are from. That is as good a beginning as any."

"I. . . . My mother was housekeeper to a country gentleman at the time I was born. . . ."

"Miss Crawley," he said in a soft but nonetheless resolute voice, "you are *not* the daughter of a housekeeper. If you continue to try and gammon me in this way I shall soon lose all patience with you.

She turned to look at him, tears trembling on her lashes. "Oh please, I beg of you, Lord Dornford, hear me out! You will understand presently, I assure you."

"Very well. Continue."

Miranda returned her attention to the handkerchief. "I have no idea who my father is or was. I believe he was a gentleman of aristocratic birth but I cannot be sure," she added quickly. "Mama always refused to discuss him with me." She stole a glance at him and with considerable relief noted no disbelief in his demeanor. "Mama's employer. . . ."

"Who is?"

"Sir Geoffrey . . . Trimm."

"I do not believe I know him."

"Do you know everyone in England, Lord Dornford?" she asked artlessly.

He smiled. "Alas, no."

"Sir Geoffrey allowed her to remain and continue as his housekeeper after I was born, which was a blessing, as you may appreciate."

She glanced at him again. He still watched her carefully, his arms folded in front of him. "Indeed," he murmured. "It was most fortunate."

"Sir Geoffrey has a daughter of his own, some three years older than I. Her own mother died in childbed and Sir Geoffrey had no mind to marry again. Therese, the daughter, looked on Mama as a substitute mother and I as a sister. Therese had a governess, of course, and we were allowed to share lessons from a very early age. Over the years we became inseparable, as sisters rarely are. That, Lord Dornford, is why I appear to be a lady of gentle birth, although it is possible my father may be well-born."

He made no comment and she went on quickly, taking a deep breath. "Eventually the inevitable happened; Therese married. By the time she returned from her honeymoon trip, Mama had taken ill with the fever and died soon after. I had hoped she would leave me some clue as to the identity of my father, but she did not. I even asked Sir Geoffrey if he could help, but all he could do was suggest one or two possibilities."

"Who are?"

"I cannot say. Sir Geoffrey informed me they were all long dead."

"How unfortunate."

When Miranda stole a glance at him again his lip was curled into almost a sneer and she continued quickly and a little breathlessly. "Therese wanted me at her new home and we were as happy as ever there until . . . until she was with child."

"And then?" the marquis gently prompted.

Miranda dabbed at her eyes. "Her husband —the squire—began to notice me."

The marquis drew in a sharp breath. "Now all is beginning to be clear." He reached for a chicken leg which he proceeded to chew thoughtfully whilst giving Miranda his full attention.

"I knew I had to get away from there; his importuning grew daily more bold. Poor Therese, if she should have learned of it, would have been devastated and I dreaded that to happen."

"Quite understandably—considering her condition."

Miranda looked to him; he appeared quite concerned, she was relieved to see.

"I decided the only course was to run away."

"I can understand your reasoning, Miss

Crawley, but did you not consider returning to the safety of Sir Geoffrey's house?"

She gave him a shocked look. "I would have had to explain my reasons. How could I tell him about the husband of his beloved Therese?"

He discarded the chicken bone and wiped his hands carefully on a linen napkin.

"And pray tell me, now that you *have* run away, what do you intend to do next? I'll wager you have not considered it."

"Once I reach London I intend to approach an agency and try to procure a position as a governess or companion. I am well-enough qualified to fulfil the requirements of either."

"With no recommendation?"

She gave him a look of disgust. "I would furnish myself with them," she answered. " 'Tis easily done."

He made a sound of annoyance and straightened up at last. "You are reckless in the extreme. You think you know every answer, but in truth you do not. Are you not aware that procuresses for the bagnios and bawdy houses scour the stagecoaches for innocents newly come to London?"

She was a little taken aback by his anger. "I know there is danger to maidens alone in the world and that is why I am dressed as a boy."

"Hah! Precious little difference that would make."

She continued to look bewildered as she

said, "Lord Dornford, I would not be so foolish as to go with one of these . . . persons. I know you regard me as scatterbrained for running away as I have, but I assure you I am held to be a very sensible female."

"They are usually kindly old ladies and you would be totally unaware of their evil until too late." He waved his hand in the air. "It is of no matter now." He turned back to the table and surveyed it quickly. "You have had no pudding. What will you have? Syllabub, blancmange, apple pie?"

"I love syllabub, but I could not possibly have any just now, I thank you. Recalling the distress of the past few months has been something of an ordeal for me and it has quite overset my feelings."

Regardless of her protest, he spooned some syllabub into a dish and when he held it out to her she could not resist. As she ate he returned to his chair, picking up his glass again. When she had finished the syllabub and a second helping too, she found he was gazing at her thoughtfully once more and gained the strange feeling that he was looking upon her kindly at last.

Slowly she said, "I trust you will not betray my confidence, Lord Dornford, and that you will allow me to continue on my journey unhindered." She paused but he made no reply and she went on, "You would . . . not think to return me to my employer?"

He put down his glass. "Oh, most certainly I would." She gasped and he went on regardless. "Your recent experience is only a foretaste of what you might yet encounter abroad alone in the world. London is a hell for innocents alone."

She lowered her eyes. "I am convinced you must be well acquainted with that fact, but be assured I will *not* be returned willy-nilly into the hands of that lecher."

His eyes filled with amusement. "I don't know whether I should be flattered by your confidence in *me*, Miss Crawley."

"Oh, I have no such confidence in you. I know you are a lecher too, Lord Dornford, and I notice that you drink. No doubt you gamble too. But I have escaped from Squire Fazackerly; now all I have to do is escape from you." She raised her chin proudly. "You would not dare to try and stop me, for I will reveal myself as a woman and you could not then pronounce me your runaway brother!"

She looked at him triumphantly, but he merely answered in the mildest tone, "Such dramatics, Miss Crawley. I have no designs on your virtue. Innocence has never attracted me." She relaxed a little although she did not quite trust him. "I have a plan which I think will suit you admirably."

She continued to look at him with hostility and suspicion as he restlessly got to his feet and took up his former position by the hearth.

He gazed down at her in silence for a moment or two and she was surprised to find that her heart was beating loudly.

"I have a sister," he said at last. "Her name is Evangeline and she is some years younger than I. This Season she has joined the ranks of those seeking a husband—in short she is making her official debut in Society. I find it a deadly bore, I admit, having often been the object of the affection of such ladies. . . ."

". . . and innocence has never attracted you."

He smiled. "Quite. We have no parents and my only surviving aunt, Lady Pendlebury, has undertaken to chaperone Evangeline and to introduce her into the correct circles but Aunt Malzena finds it something of a bore to be constantly with a young girl. *She* prefers her card parties and her own cronies. This, Miss Crawley, is where I believe you can help. I wish to engage you as my sister's companion."

Miranda was taken aback and looked it, but was allowed to make no comment. "You can listen to her brainless prattle, go shopping with her, help her dress and so on, and all for—say—ten guineas a year. Does the prospect appeal to you, Miss Crawley?"

"No," she said at last.

"Why ever not? It is precisely the type of position you are seeking, or am I mistaken in that assumption?"

"I couldn't possibly. . . ."

One eyebrow went up a fraction. "I am still waiting to hear your reasons. Perhaps you would prefer a schoolroom brat."

Miranda continued to pull unconsciously at the handkerchief. "You misunderstand my hesitation. . . ." She looked up at him. "You only have my word for what I am. As you so rightly pointed out I have no letter to recommend me."

"Miss Crawley, you accused me of having no heart, but your story has truly distressed me."

She looked to him for signs of levity but found none. "If I have done you an injustice, my lord. . . ."

"No, I beg of you, no apologies. Let us say we have come to the aid of each other with no cause for gratitude on either side.

"I am willing to engage you on at least a trial basis, but 'tis true I may be the only one prepared to do so. I will be honest with you, Miss Crawley, my sister although empty-headed is thought to be quite handsome and that together with her not inconsiderable portion will ensure that she has ensnared some besotted fool before the Season is ended."

Miranda found that her anger towards him was kindling within her breast once more. "You are undoubtedly, Lord Dornford, a disagreeable man to hold such a low opinion of your own sister."

"You do me an injustice; I am truly fond of the chit but I am merely pointing out to you the virtues of the position. If you can bear to accompany my sister to all the fashionable emporiums, ride with her in the park—I take it you do ride . . .?" She nodded and he went on, "Attend various balls and routs with her, then by the time she is married I shall be able to furnish you with a recommendation which will open any door to you. You will be able to pick and choose your next position, I promise you."

She bit her lip thoughtfully. Her momentary panic at being trapped was gone, and she quickly evaluated the offer, realising in amazement that this could be just what she needed. In fact, it could scarcely be better.

"Of course, you could always return to your former post," the marquis added. "That is, you understand, the alternative, for I could not in all conscience leave you to your own devices in London."

"Oh, I am sensible of the advantage of your offer, Lord Dornford," she hastened to assure him, "and I was not seeking to refuse, I was merely wondering if I am well enough qualified for the position you offer."

"Then tell me what are your accomplishments, although I assure you, you will need little save a head for listening to idle chatter."

"I sew a little, I can dress hair tolerably well, play the harpsichord, read quite pleasingly. . . ."

He held up his hand. "Enough! Enough, Miss Crawley. 'Tis indeed too much. You will spoil Evangeline so much she may insist, like the unfortunate Mrs Fazackerly, on having you with her even after she is married."

Miranda averted her pink cheeks and asked in a strangled voice, "May I ask if she has a beau?"

"Scores of them, Miss Crawley, and new ones being added to her conquests each week. I fear that Lady Pendlebury will be quite done up if relief is not to hand soon."

He cleared his throat. "I trust you have some . . . female apparel amongst your baggage. . . .?"

"Yes, yes, indeed. I have a gown with me."

"Naturally you will wear it when you accompany me into town on the morrow. You may leave the coat and breeches where they fall—unless you wish to return them to their owner."

Miranda digested this slowly. "The clothes were long ago abandoned by one of the squire's relatives."

"You do not surprise me at all," he answered laconically.

"Where shall I spend tonight?" she hesitated to ask.

"Here, of course. I have no mind to travel these roads at night unless it is a matter of life and death, and now we have disposed of the god-mother in Paddington I trust that it is not." He ignored the unbecoming flush which was once more creeping up her cheeks. "I have

taken the liberty of bespeaking a bedchamber
for you." She almost choked at the reminder of
the previous evening, but he appeared not to
notice her embarrassment. "Tonight, I promise you, you will have a room of your own, Miss
Crawley. Had I known. . . . Well, tomorrow be
pleased to appear in your gown. I do not wish
my aunt and sister to die of fright." He took
out his time-piece and glanced at it. "I believe
it is time we both retired. The room I have re-
served for you, you will find far more comfortable than that at the 'Bell'. It will mean an
early start again in the morning if we are to be
in London by nightfall and I advise you to get
as much rest as you can."

"That is advice I shall readily follow."

She quickly got to her feet, glad to be dis-
missed at last. She needed solitude now to consider her milling thoughts and put them into
order. Even now she was not sure she had done
the right thing in accepting this post, although
there had been little choice for her. Something
told her this man was not the benefactor he
pretended to be. A marquis he might be and
wealthy too, but Miranda was well aware such
men could be and often were as wicked as those
of less elevated lineage. It was a chance she
would have to take.

When she reached the door she paused to
glance back at him. She was not surprised to
find that he was studying her.

A little uncertainly she said, "Goodnight, Lord Dornford."

He inclined his head slightly, but before he did she could see the look of malicious amusement in his eyes and it disturbed her but he merely said, "Good night to you, Miss Crawley," and she hurried from the room.

Chapter Three

Miranda gazed out of the window of Lord Dornford's travelling carriage and her eyes grew wide with all she saw. She knew London to be a large town and that there was much to wonder at, but she had never imagined there to be so many people, fine buildings, nor so many shops.

Their journey from the inn had been a swift and comfortable one, a direct contrast to the earlier part of her flight to London. When she had come down from her bedchamber that morning, she was still not sure about the marquis's motives and the night's rest had not made anything clearer. She realised she was not likely to find out so easily, for he was a strange man although his cynicism might well only be a mask.

The stagecoach travellers were about to depart and Miranda was tempted to rejoin them and risk all the dire perils the marquis had pointed out. It amused her that none of her travelling companions of the previous day recognised her. On an impulse she went towards them, thinking there might be more safety in numbers than that dubiously offered by the marquis, but as she passed the private parlour the door was standing open and Lord Dornford was already at the table having his breakfast, which made her wonder if he might have been waiting for her whatever hour she had chosen to rise. He saw her immediately, of course, and called her in, and she bowed to the inevitability of fate.

In accordance with his instructions, Myles's old coat and breeches lay on the bedroom floor. On this morning she wore a gown of green watered silk, some two years old, and a bergere hat which was even older but the only one she possessed that was small enough to pack in a cloakbag.

She had hesitated in the doorway, waiting for some comment on her appearance and although he did cast a very critical eye over her he merely said, "Pray, sit down, Miss Crawley, and have your breakfast. We have no time to delay."

Afterwards she wondered what she had expected him to say, for her gown was shabby and her appearance unremarkable in every way. A man such as the Marquis of Dornford would be acquainted with the most beautiful and fashionable ladies in the land, and Miranda dared not imagine how she would compare to them.

During the journey he talked to her infrequently, save on their stop for dinner, but she did not really mind; she enjoyed being accorded all the ceremony due to someone travelling with a marquis, and her own suppressed excitement and milling thoughts connected with her imminent arrival in London were sufficient to keep her well occupied.

Now, after crossing the river and passing through central London, the chaise had entered the Oxford Road. Shops abounded here, a fairyland of bright lights illuminating dazzling arrays of jewellery, clocks, pastries, silks and taffetas, and bottles of brightly coloured liquids in apothecary shops, all displayed behind bow windows.

The pavements thronged with the most sumptuously dressed people Miranda had ever seen. There were poorly dressed people too but she scarcely noticed them. Nothing so far disappointed her; everything was as wonderful—if not more so—than she had imagined. There were a great many elegant town carriages, curricles and phaetons—many emblazoned with aristocratic crests—lining each side of the road and even down the middle. Coachmen stood in groups talking amongst themselves or walking up and down to keep warm. In their coloured liveries they alone made a splendid sight on which a stranger could feast her eyes.

The chaise had bowled along at a fast pace for most of the day and it would be hours yet before the stagecoach would reach its destination. Having used both modes of travelling Miranda could now understand the marquis's advantage but now because of the density of the traffic the chaise could only move at a snail's pace.

The marquis, who since their stop for dinner had been concentrating on a number of papers bound up in a portfolio, now looked up and Miranda took the opportunity of asking:

"Are we far from our destination, Lord Dornford?"

The bruise was still livid on his cheek and this together with the scar on his other cheek gave him a rakish and slightly sinister appearance. Miranda wondered if the duel in which he had received the scar had been over some beautiful woman.

The marquis glanced out of the carriage window and displayed no particular interest at what he saw. "My house is in Portman Square, which is not far from here."

"Is the Oxford Road always as busy as this?"

"It is always busy, but today delays are inevitable. It is execution day at Tyburn and the riff-raff from miles around have been here to see the entertainment."

Miranda's eyes clouded. "Entertainment! Who can consider it so?"

"Many people do. At Tyburn it is a great occasion, almost like a fair."

"Oh, how terrible! I hope we shall not have to see it."

"Indeed not, Miss Crawley. We shall leave this thoroughfare before we reach the Tyburn gibbet."

She shuddered, aware that he was watching her with scarce concealed amusement. "Once when I was young a footpad was hanged near my home," she told him. "We had no alternative but to drive past the gibbet on our way into town. His body was left there for several weeks and we were obliged to avert our eyes each time we passed. It was quite dreadful. I had nightmares about it for weeks."

He smiled. "That is the idea, Miss Crawley. These creatures are left as an awful warning to others not to stray from the paths of righteousness."

Miranda sat up straight and said huffily, "As none of our household were like to become footpads, I cannot see the right of that, my lord."

At this point the carriage left the main thoroughfare and passed into a blessedly quieter one. A few minutes later the chaise turned into a beautiful square surrounded by elegant town houses. As she was helped down from the chaise outside Lord Dornford's house Miranda glanced around her with interest. The house itself was pleasing enough, with sash windows, a portico and a fanlight over the door, but it was not as large as she had imagined it would be.

However, as she entered the hall, paved in black and white marble, she had an agreeable surprise, for it was far larger than it appeared from the outside. A curving staircase led to the upper floors with candelabra on each newel post, and the walls adorned by paintings alternating with alcoves filled with Italian statuary of great beauty. The ceilings were heavily gilded and a satinwood chiffonier stood in one corner filled with Dresden shepherdesses of varying styles and sizes. There seemed to be a prodigious number of doors leading off the hall and Miranda feared she might easily lose her way until she grew accustomed to the plan of the house.

The marquis handed his greatcoat to the house steward whilst a liveried footman in blue and gold relieved Miranda of her pelisse which was looking shabbier all the time.

"Is Lady Pendlebury at home?" the marquis enquired.

"Yes, my lord," the steward answered, allowing his curious gaze to stray to Miranda for a moment. "In the small drawing room."

The marquis indicated to Miranda that she was to follow him up the stairs and at this point she was once again assailed by doubts, but when he paused halfway up to wait for her she hurriedly followed.

An attendant footman flung open the doors at the top of the stairs and she followed the marquis into a drawing room done out in the Chinese style which she admired so much. Laquered cabinets filled with fine china stood around the walls, the silk wallhangings displayed a willow pattern and even the sofas had armpieces in the shape of dragon's heads.

Miranda was so fascinated by the decor of the room she did not notice the lady who was reclining on a day bed near a blazing fire until she moved.

"James! My dear boy, you're home again. How glad I am to see you!"

Miranda immediately transferred her attention to the rather large lady who clutched at the marquis's hands. The resemblance was rather startling to say the least. Lady Pendlebury was also dark and well built and both were equally imposing in looks. Lady Pendlebury wore a muslin mob cap over her hair and a gown almost as outmoded as Miranda's own.

"You must tell me all about your journey," Lady Pendlebury was saying. "Have you concluded the purchase of the land?"

"We can speak of it later, Aunt Malzena, but first tell me if Evangeline is at home?"

"She should be arriving at any moment now. Mr. Romney has agreed to paint her portrait. Since you have been away from home Evangeline has had three sittings."

"That is excellent news, aunt, but surely,"

he asked, frowning now, "she is not out on her own."

Lady Pendlebury laughed. "She was accompanied by her maid and a footman." She put one hand to her head. "I just could not face leaving the house today."

He smiled suddenly and his face was devoid of irony. He looked quite natural to Miranda and much younger than before and she thought it a pity he was not more often like it.

"A card evening last night, aunt?"

"At Bess Carleton's, but don't ask me your next question, I beg of you. I did not play too deep."

"That is something of a novelty." He stood to one side. "Aunt Malzena, I have a surprise for you and Evangeline. I have brought someone to bear her company, which should relieve you a little of your responsibility."

Lady Pendlebury, who had so far been unaware of Miranda's presence just inside the doorway, turned on her heel and her eyes opened wide.

"Who is this?"

The marquis beckoned her further into the room and she came forward rather timidly, clutching at her hat which she had removed on entering the house. She was well-aware of how inconspicuous she looked in her outmoded gown and with her hair tumbling from its pins.

"Allow me to introduce Miss Miranda Crawley to you, aunt."

Miranda recovered her wits sufficiently to bob a curtsey but Lady Pendlebury did not acknowledge the introduction; she merely rounded on her nephew. "Really, James, what are you up to?"

The marquis looked both amused and taken aback. "Up to, Aunt Malzena? What should I be up to? Miss Crawley is here to benefit both Evangeline and yourself. I thought you would be pleased."

Lady Pendlebury put one hand up to stop him. "Nonsense, boy. What a ridiculous idea! A companion for Evangeline. Does she not have enough companionship already?"

Miranda began to back out of the room again, putting the hat back on and tying the ribbons with trembling fingers. "I quite understand, Lady Pendlebury," she said breathlessly. "I need not stay if you do not wish it."

Before she had gone more than a few steps the marquis had crossed the room in three strides and caught her by the arm. "Aunt Malzena, only think; with Miss Crawley here you can be free to enjoy your own pursuits much more than you are able at present."

Lady Pendlebury's eyes narrowed suspiciously. "Who is the girl? Where did you find her?"

Miranda looked at him in alarm, but he was totally unperturbed. Smilingly he explained. "Miss Crawley was lately in the employ of

Squire Fazackerly. One cannot have a better recommendation than that."

The look of suspicion went from the old lady's face. "Ah, Squire Fazackerly. Why did you not say so immediately?" And then, addressing Miranda for the first time she smiled, "My dear, let me apologise for my boorish behaviour. My only excuse is that my rascally newphew is constantly springing odd surprises on me, and this certainly is, if not the oddest, the most unexpected."

She looked at her nephew again. "I am sure there is much sense in what you say and I am also quite certain you are longing to be away to your business, so off with you whilst Miss Crawley and I take tea together and become better acquainted."

The marquis let her arm go at last and smiled down at her. It was not a benevolent smile, but one which discomforted her greatly. "I leave you in good hands."

With that he was gone from the room and as much as she feared and distrusted him she missed his presence now. His aunt could be a good deal worse.

Lady Pendlebury ushered her to a sofa. Miranda approached it slowly, afraid that this rather garrulous lady might ask a great many questions she would rather not answer. As astute as Lord Dornford had been, women were famous for ferreting out all manner of things.

But she need not have feared; Lady Pendlebury, for the halfhour that followed, herself talked almost without pause, giving Miranda no opportunity to give away any secrets.

They had just finished tea when the doors burst open and in rushed the most exquisite creature Miranda had ever set eyes upon. Lady Evangeline Devilliars had inherited the dark looks of her family, but she was as dainty as a doll. The marquis certainly did not do his sister justice in his description of her.

"Aunt Malzena! Is Dornford home at last?"

"Yes, dear. Isn't that splendid? Come along in and tell me all about your afternoon."

Evangeline saw Miranda then and looked uncertain. "Oh, I am sorry to have burst in like this, aunt. I didn't know you had a visitor."

"That's quite all right, dear. Tell me, how was the sitting?"

Her face dimpled as she came further into the room. "It went splendidly. At first I was horribly afraid of sitting for so illustrious a man, but he couldn't have been more charming. Mr. Romney actually said it was an honour for him to paint my portrait as he rarely had so fair a subject, and he praised me too for sitting so still. He said I'd be surprised to know how many fidgets there were. Imagine, Aunt Malzena! To say such things to me after painting so many Beauties."

"I am sure he would not say it if it were not true."

"Where is Dornford? He has surely not gone out already."

"He will be along shortly. This is Miss Crawley, Evangeline. James has engaged her to be your companion."

The girl's sunny smile faded as she looked properly at Miranda at last. "This is a jest, aunt. A companion? Oh, no." She looked in distress at her aunt. "I don't want a companion. You must see that this is only a ruse so James can spy on me. I know it!"

"Such dramatics, Evangeline," came a soothing and faintly mocking voice from the doorway. "You would do well at Drury Lane, my dear."

She turned on her heel and faced her brother angrily. "How dare you do this to me. It is not to be borne!"

She stamped her foot and his indulgent smile faded. "This is not the place to indulge in one of your miffs. Be pleased to come into the library." He glanced across at his aunt. "In the meanwhile, Aunt Malzena, perhaps you would be good enough to show Miss Crawley her room. I am sure she would welcome a rest before supper."

For one moment it looked as though the girl was about to refuse but her brother did not wait for an answer, and flashing one furious look in Miranda's direction she flounced out of the room after him.

Lady Pendlebury sighed deeply. "Headstrong," she murmured. "It is a failing of the entire family, I regret to say."

Miranda was alarmed. "I do hope Lord Dornford isn't going to bully her into accepting me. That would not do at all."

The old lady smiled. "Oh, so you have already discovered my nephew can be something of a bully. He does manage to do it in a gentle way though." Miranda did not trouble to contradict her on this point. "It is, of course, the penalty of his being an only son. He was petted and spoiled by both his parents, especially my sister. She had several miscarriages before James was born and afterwards too. It undermined her health, you know, and consequently she did not survive long after Evangeline was born, and then, of course, *she* was spoiled too. I regard it as a blessing I did not have any children. It is all I can do to control my sister's."

She got heavily to her feet. "Come along, child. I will take you upstairs. You look quite exhausted as well you might after such an arduous journey. Do not heed Evangeline. She is really quite a sweet child and will grow used to the idea of having you around her."

"I hope you may be right, Lady Pendlebury," Miranda murmured as they left the room, "otherwise it will be very uncomfortable for us all, I fancy. I did not think it a good idea when Lord Dornford suggested it. She is rather young to be in need of a companion."

"I deem it a good idea. You will have much in common."

It was growing dark and candle sconces and chandeliers were being lit all over the house by the servants. Miranda had never seen such an amount of candles and she dreaded to think what Lord Dornford's chandler's bill would be.

As they climbed the stairs a footman followed holding up a many-branched candelabrum to make their way the lighter. When they reached the next floor Lady Pendlebury was quite out of breath.

"Do you know what the Dornford family motto is?" she asked as the footman flung open the door. Miranda shook her head. "*Resolute in all things.* It really is an apt motto, for my nephew is a very resolute person when he so chooses. His father was much the same. It may help you understand a little."

She could not help but laugh. The footman put down the branch of candles and proceeded to light the wall sconces. A fire was blazing in the hearth, throwing a flickering light over the room which was of ample proportions, as was the bed with its silk tester and counterpane.

"What a delightful room!" Miranda exclaimed.

Lady Pendlebury hurried to the door. "The sheets have been warmed and aired, have no fear, and do not be afraid to ring if there is anything you want. The servants are by and large as good as one can get, but tend to excuse themselves their duties if they think they can get away with it. You are situated not far from my niece's apartment. Supper will be served in an hour so you have ample time to rest and prepare yourself. You may consider it fortunate we have no guests tonight."

Miranda was quick to agree on that point and when she was left alone at last she sank wearily onto a sofa in front of the fire. She looked down at her gown, knowing it would be sadly inadequate for life in the Dornford house. What sufficed the Sussex gentry would certainly not do here. She would need more clothes and there was only one place she could go for money to buy them. That would be an easy task; the problem was, how to explain them away.

With a sigh Miranda looked around her at last, reflecting that the marquis certainly lived in considerable style if this were merely a guest room. A French secretaire stood in one corner and a clothes press in another. Suddenly she noticed that hot water had been placed in the washstand and she quickly removed her clothes and washed herself thoroughly, removing, she hoped, most of the grime of the journey.

Later, standing in her petticoats, after rearranging her hair and repowdering it she suddenly realised that come what may she was in London—her goal for the past three years. London. As Lady Evangeline Devilliars's companion every kind of high-flown social activity would be hers to enjoy. The unfortunate encounter with the marquis had turned into the most remarkable stroke of luck.

She began to laugh at the irony of the situation and then danced round the room with sheer joy until someone knocked on the door. She froze and the knock came again.

She called out, "One minute please," and struggled into her gown. Smoothing down the skirt she invited in a muted voice, "Come in."

A moment later Lady Evangeline stood framed in the doorway. "May I come in?" she asked hesitantly.

Equally hesitantly Miranda answered, "Of course," and closed the door behind her. "Won't you sit down, Lady Evangeline?"

The girl did so, asking, "I trust you have been made comfortable."

"Very much so."

She patted the sofa seat. "Miss Crawley, will you join me and let us have a coze?" Intrigued, Miranda sat down at her side and she went on quickly, "I wish to apologise for my boorish behaviour earlier."

Miranda was indeed taken aback for this was not at all what she had expected. "Lady Evangeline, you have no need. If you do not wish to have a companion I fully. . . ."

The girl shook her head. "The truth of matter is I have never *considered* the possibility. Now that I have had time the idea seems to me to be an admirable one. I was thoughtless, Miss Crawley. My brother has acquainted me with your circumstances. . . ."

As Miranda's eyes opened wide with surprise and alarm the girl held up one dainty hand. "I realise what you told him was in the deepest confidence but I assure you that not a word of it will pass my lips—not even under pain of death."

Miranda stared into the leaping flames which she hoped would disguise her crimson cheeks. "I . . . I am obliged."

"Miss Crawley," she went on in earnest, "I am addicted to as many novels as I can borrow from Mr. Pomeroy's Circulating Library and yet in all their pages I have never read a more heartrending story. The agony you must have endured—the divided loyalty. . . ."

Miranda was sure she could bear no more and turned to Lady Evangeline. "Oh please, I beg of you say no more! The very memory of it causes me untold agony."

There were actually tears in the girl's eyes as she put on hand over Miranda's arm. "Forgive me; I have been thoughtless once again. You have my word on it; it will never be mentioned between us again. You must strive to forget the unhappiness in your past."

"Does that mean . . . you wish me to remain?"

Lady Evangeline clasped her hands to her bosom. "Oh yes, Miss Crawley, but not just as my paid companion. My brother, I know, has come to some financial arrangement with you, but as far as I am concerned you will be here as my bosom friend."

Miranda was moved beyond words and close to tears herself. She no longer considered her luck but her good fortune. This girl was so naive and so trusting it put her in an impossible position. Had she proved to be the spoiled brat she initially appeared or the selfish and vain harpy Miranda had envisaged, the hoax would have been easy to continue, and even enjoy. But now.. . . She felt wretched and was tempted to leave Dornford House before she sank further into this imbroglio.

"Now," Lady Evangeline said in a more brisk voice, "may I call you Miranda? It is such a pretty name."

"Of course," she answered in a husky voice. "I should be glad of it."

"And you must, naturally, call me Evangeline."

"I couldn't," Miranda protested in shocked tones. "It wouldn't be right."

The girl's eyes sparkled. "I insist. You cannot refuse." Miranda nodded and she went on, "I understand you escaped with only a few clothes, Miranda."

"That is true. This is my only gown and I fear it is shabby."

Evangleine got to her feet. "That is a matter easily remedied, my dear. I shall simply ask

Dornford for sufficient funds to provide you with everything you require."

Miranda was horrified. "Oh please, I beg of you, do not. I would die of mortification."

"Such pride," she murmured admiringly and then her lovely face puckered into a frown. "Then what are you to do?"

Miranda brightened. The answer was a simple one. "You must surely have gowns that you have discarded; I am held to be quite accomplished with the needle. I can soon adapt them for my own use and no one would be the wiser."

"Is it possible to modernise outmoded gowns?"

"It is an easy task."

The girl clapped her hands. "How clever you are! There are dozens of gowns all packed away in trunks, some of them belonged to Mama. I will have the servants bring them to you immediately and you shall choose as many as you want."

"I am obliged to you."

"I only wish *I* was clever with the needle. Aunt Malzena is forever admonishing me for my clumsy stitches. I cannot even sew my stockings and none of the maidservants can darn."

"I shall do them all for you—and do them well, I promise you."

Evangeline's face dimpled. "You are a dear. I am going to love having you here. I was so in need of companionship; Dornford is so clever to know it. Now we must hurry or we'll be late for supper."

Evangeline hurried her out of the room and as she did so Miranda could not help but remark, "Surely you don't really need me as a confidante, much as I value your friendship. You must have many friends of your own circle."

"I do, but there is not one I can confide in. They are all jealous, you see, because I have so many *beaux*. At least six have offered for me and the season is not even half over yet."

"Did you not want to accept any of them?" Miranda asked in astonishment.

"Not one out of two earls, one duke, three viscounts and an heir to a baronet."

"But surely Lord Dornford must have advised. . . .?"

"Oh no. Dornford says the choice is entirely mine and informed every suitor of the fact."

"I can understand why you are envied, Evangeline. I am also in awe of you."

The girl laughed. "Those creatures can be as mean as toads and often look like one too. When I wear rouge they say I look flushed and when I do not they say I look pale."

Miranda chuckled. "They have a little of my sympathy, Evangeline. You must be a formidable rival."

Evangeline squeezed her arm playfully but all girlish conversation ceased as they went to join Lord Dornford and Lady Pendlebury for supper. Throughout the meal Miranda flashed angry looks across the table at him for telling his sister that tale of woe, but he did not appear to have noticed it. For the most part he chatted to his sister, who, Miranda was surprised to note, looked upon him adoringly, and Miranda's own attention was taken by Lady Pendlebury who chattered inconsequentially with scarcely a pause for breath. Her capacity to consume large amounts of food at the same time amazed Miranda who could only admire her for it.

It was not until the marquis joined them in the drawing room for tea that she had the opportunity to say, "Shame on you, Lord Dornford, for betraying my confidence to your sister."

He merely smiled as he took a pinch of snuff and looked not the least bit troubled by the stricture. "I regret the necessity as much as you, Miss Crawley, but the information had the effect no amount of insistence and strictures on my part would do."

She could not dispute it. "But it is such a shameful story."

"I agree," he answered mildly.

"I trust you did not also reveal," she said stiffly, "the circumstances of our initial meeting." Despite herself her cheeks grew warm at the recollection.

He gave her a look of mock horror. "Miss Crawley, I have my reputation to consider,"

and then he added in a more normal tone,
"Have no fear, neither my sister nor myself
will mention it again."

"I have your sister's word."

"And mine as a gentleman. The incident is
forgotten."

She raised her eyes to his and knew he was
not mocking her this time.

"What are you two talking about so earnestly?" Evangline laughingly asked as she came
across the room towards them.

The marquis quickly got to his feet and said
in a low voice to Miranda before his sister was
close enough to hear, "Everything is settled
admirably, my dear. Here you are, Miss Crawley, and here you will stay."

And as his sister approached them, he sauntered away.

Chapter Four

For the best part of the ensuing week Miranda
was kept busy preparing a suitable wardrobe
as befitted her new role in life. As promised,
the chests were delivered to her room early the
following day and she found them to be filled
with a wonderful assortment of silks, velvets,
satins and brocades, which would be a delight
to handle let alone to wear. Miranda knew she
would enjoy making the necessary alterations
and working on such exquisite materials. She
could scarcely wait to finish the first polonaise
gown of blue watered silk, her favourite mate-
rial. When it was finished, she vowed to herself, it would look as good as any worn by the
ladies of the *ton*.

During this time she saw little of the marquis, even at meal times, for it transpired that
he was often out of the house. It was something of a relief and yet in a strange way she
missed his presence when he was not there.

There was an odd kind of enjoyment to be derived from their gentle duels of words.

Both Lady Pendlebury and Evangeline had many engagements to fulfil, which for the moment left Miranda free to sew. Every day, though, Evangeline insisted on seeing the results of her work and exclaimed constantly how clever she was, much to Miranda's embarrassment.

Not that she was entirely confined to Dornford House during this period; almost every day Evangeline sallied forth on shopping expeditions, and whilst the infinite variety of the emporiums and the sheer splendour of the goods fascinated and excited Miranda, she could easily understand Lady Pendlebury wishing for respite. Evangeline scoured the mercers in Pall Mall for new cloths imported from France, India or China, and bought ribbons and laces, all of which were miraculously transformed by the mantua-maker into gorgeous gowns. She bought her favourite rosewater in Bond Street and selected hats at a milliner's whose shop was situated in the Strand. Miranda had to admit she had rarely enjoyed herself more.

There was a constant stream of callers to the house, some of whom she caught sight of from time to time; ladies and gentlemen arriving in smart carriages, people so obviously of great consequence. Each time she passed through the main hall there was a pile of calling cards left in the silver salver on a table near the door, not to mention posies of flowers, boxes of marchpane and sweetmeats from some of Evangeline's legion of admirers. Such a sight often brought a feeling of longing to Miranda's heart; she so badly wanted to see Cornelius but she must needs seek out Myles first, and she vowed to do so at the earliest opportunity.

The opportunity did not arise until almost a week had passed after her arrival. It was intended that she always accompany Evangeline to her sitting with the painter George Romney, but they were also attending the Haymarket Theatre that evening for a new production of *The Beggar's Opera*. It was to be Miranda's first engagement in public and she was feverishly trying to finish a gown fit for the occasion. Realising this, Evangeline insisted that she take her maid instead on this occasion.

The gown needed little more sewing and Miranda soon had it completed to her satisfaction. When it was finished her eyes were tired but the afternoon stretched long before her and it didn't take much time for her to decide how to use it.

She changed into a gown of pomona green silk with a fine gauze tippet folded across the bosom. Over it she put her own velvet pelisse and hurried out of the house. There was a feeling of suppressed excitement inside her at the thought of being out alone at last in the town.

She managed to engage a sedan chair at the

corner of the square and charged the chairmen to take her to the St. James's address written on the piece of paper in her pocket. It seemed only a short time later that she was let down on the pavement outside the very address she was seeking. She paid the chairmen and added a small vail with which they seemed satisfied.

The moment she was set down a match-girl came hurrying up to her, showing her wares and entreating her to buy. Amidst the riches Miranda had often seen, she had as frequently been repelled by the grinding poverty of so many others, and this girl was no exception. Match-thin herself, she was clothed in no more than rags; certainly not enough to keep out the winter cold. Miranda did not want her matches but nevertheless pressed sixpence into her hand. When the girl began to thank her profusely Miranda waved her away in embarrassment and then hesitated on the pavement gazing up at the lodging house which was her destination.

The brass plate by the door, the knocker and door knob were all highly polished and the house was obviously a well-kept one. There was a railing outside dividing the cellar from the street. Barrels of ale were being rolled off a handcart into the cellar of the house next door and the draymen were making a great deal of noise about it.

After a few moments Miranda approached the house and knocked on the door. Her sum-

mons was answered by a fresh-faced maidservant who looked at her expectantly.

"Is Mr. Templeton at home?" she demanded
immediately.

"No, ma'am, he is not."

Miranda felt a stab of disappointment but
no real surprise. "Do you expect him back
soon?"

The girl smiled. "I expect so ma'am."

"I'm his sister. I have come a long way to see
him and it is rather important."

"In that case, ma'am, mayhap you'd care to
wait in the parlour."

Miranda stepped over the threshold thankfully and the maid ushered her into a spotless
parlour. The maid withdrew immediately and
Miranda seated herself by the window where
she could watch people passing by and hopefully see Myles the moment he returned to his
lodgings.

Despite the vast amount of shops there
seemed to be in London, there were also many
goods sold by hawkers in the streets. The air
was constantly filled by their individual cries
which was a direct contrast to the country
quiet to which Miranda was used. A pie-man
passed by the window and his wares looked delicious but she was far too excited to stop him.
Mingling with the elegantly-dressed ladies and
gentlemen passing by were footmen and maids
on errands for their masters and an orange-
seller and a sweep passed by before Miranda

realised she had been sitting there for some time. She hoped Myles would return to his lodgings soon, for she dared not stay out too long and it would be too cruel to have to return to Dornford House without seeing him on this occassion.

A man with an ass passed by to be stopped by a finely dressed gentleman who passed a few coins to the fellow. The owner of the ass immediately began to milk the creature and the customer downed his drink before continuing on his way.

Suddenly the door burst open. Miranda turned and then jumped to her feet at the sight of the fashionable young man who had burst in.

"Myles! Oh, Myles!"

"Miranda. What the devil. . . .?"

She flew into his arms and was for the moment so overcome with emotion she could not speak. After a moment or two he held her away.

"What a wonderful surprise. I can't tell you how splendid it is to see you. In truth, I can scarce believe it."

She laughed unevenly. "Nor I." She straightened his wig which she had inadvertently tipped.

"You look magnificent. I have never seen you wearing that gown before. How is it you're here? Who has brought you?" She looked away, no longer able to meet his eyes. "How did you persuade Papa to let you leave him?"

"I didn't," she said in a small voice. "At least, not to come here."

Myles came towards her, looking at her questioningly. "Miranda? You haven't . . . run away, have you?"

She turned back to him then, looking at him with beseeching eyes. "Not quite. Papa thinks me to be in Cheltenham with Lucy Ferrier, my old school friend. He does not care, Myles," she said with sudden bitterness. "He cares only for his books, as well you know. He will not even notice I am gone! When I set out for London I admit I did fear that he might discover my duplicity and send a Runner after me, but I should have known better. I had nothing to fear from him."

"But much from other quarters, I'll have you know."

"I am here, dearest, and unharmed as you can plainly see."

Scratching his head he said in a bemused voice, "Sit down. Sit down, and let us talk." He too sat down and, leaning forward, asked, "How did you get here? Post chaise?"

Miranda swallowed noisily. "It is a very long tale, Myles."

She began to tell him about her journey which he immediately interrupted by exclaiming, "By stage, Miranda! Ye Gods. If only I had known."

"I had only pin money by me. I scraped together what I could and knew it was enough to get me here safely, after which you could supply me with all the funds I need."

He fumbled with his purse and brought out a few gold sovereigns which he held out to her. "It is all I have at the moment, but it will be enough to keep by you in case of need."

"I don't want to take your last sovereigns, Myles."

"Take them," he insisted. "I can always beg the blunt until I have a chance to draw some more."

Gratefully she pocketed the money. It was possible to manage with little or no money in the country, but for her it was frustrating in London where there was so much to tempt her in the shops, although she was well aware she must spend sparingly lest she arouse suspicion.

She took a deep breath and began to tell him about her meeting with Lord Dornford, omitting, naturally, the fact that it took place in a bedchamber and anything else which would outrage his sensibilities.

"The Marquis of Dornford!" he cried, jumping to his feet. "That rake! How could you, Miranda?"

"He has behaved with perfect propriety, Myles," she said primly, averting her face so that he could not see her cheeks which had grown quite pink. "Indeed, you have cause to thank him."

His face suddenly brightened. "Did Dornford really believe that Banbury Tale you told him?"

Miranda laughed delightedly. "Every word. I swear there was a tear in his eye."

Her brother laughed heartily for a moment or two. "That is famous. His reputation is not one for being kind, let me assure you." And then he became troubled once more. "But for you to be employed by him. My sister; Sir William Templeton's daughter."

"He does not know that and neither does anyone else."

"Indeed, I hope not! You have adopted another name I trust. Papa would not welcome scandal attached to his name."

"I am known as Miss Crawley."

"Miss Crawley," he repeated. "Is there some significance in that?"

"It was merely the first name which came into my head, but," she added, grinning mischievously, "it is suited to a paid companion, don't you think? Very often they are obliged to crawl." At the look of dismay on his face she quickly added, "Do not concern yourself on my account. I am perfectly content for the moment."

"But if anyone were to find out. . . ."

"Only you and I know. When Evangeline marries—as the marquis earnestly expects before the Season is over—I shall merely return home and no one will be the wiser and in the meantime I shall be enjoying all the fun London has to offer. It is a splendid ruse."

"I don't like it. You must return home immediately. I insist upon it."

"No," she said resolutely. "You cannot make me. If you try you will only make yourself look ridiculous if it becomes known I ran away from home to become a paid companion to Lady Evangeline Devilliars. Myles, just admit, you cannot do anything about it."

He seemed to crumple back into the chair. "Why have you come, Miranda? Why?"

She began to wring her hands together at the sight of his anguish. "I did truly think you would be glad to see me."

"And so I am, but in these circumstances. . . ."

"Myles, I just could not bear to be incarcerated in the country any longer. It isn't fair that I should; you are my twin and yet I must remain at home whilst you are free to do as you please."

"I am a man, and you did not object when I went to Eton and on my Grand Tour."

"This is quite different. Oh, dearest, please understand. Living at home was not like living at all. I read magazines showing the latest fashions, knowing I should never have an opportunity to wear them. Father is so odd, no one comes to call. I shall never have an opportunity to marry let alone have friends of my own age. There is, of course, Mr. Failston," she added in bitter tones, "he's the new curate. He comes to call on Father to discuss his writings of late and I do not like the looks he has been casting in my direction."

"I will deal with the impudent puppy if that is all which troubles you. Have no fear of that, Miranda."

"Oh, Mr. Failston has never overstepped the bounds, but if he were to ask for permission to pay his addresses to me Papa is like to give it him. They get on famously, but he is such a prosy bore and has bad teeth and pimples. I don't like him at all."

"As Evangeline Devilliars' companion did you imagine you will have a chance to marry?"

"That is not my object although she has adopted me as her bosom friend."

He leaned forward. "Oh, Miranda," he sighed, "why are you so impetuous? Once I am settled with a wife *she* would present you to Society in the proper way and you would have the social life you wish."

She shook her head. "It will be too late. I am already turned twenty.

"Myles," she added in a soft voice, "there is more to the matter than I have yet told you. Although it is true having you home this summer—just as it was when we were children—was a marvellous thing, and when you went away the house seemed more empty than before, but this time it was different. You had brought Mr. Osborne with you."

Miranda stared at her gloves which lay in her lap as her brother got slowly to his feet again. "Cornelius? What has he to do with it?"

In exasperation she laughed. "Oh, dearest, you are quite obtuse. I am in love with him."

The young man had gone quite white. "Well, if that doesn't beat the dutch! I had no idea."

"Didn't he mention me to you at all?"

"Naturally. I am well aware he holds you in the greatest esteem." His eyes narrowed. "Has he been filling you with flummery, Miranda?"

She shook her head dreamily. "Mr. Osborne has acted always with perfect propriety. It was a gradual awareness of each other. When you both left I knew I would lose him if I did not remain in his life." Myles Templeton passed a weary hand across his face as his sister asked, "You will tell him I am here?"

He nodded. "Yes, I will tell him, but I know he will be as outraged as I am. Miranda, are you sure you haven't mistaken his kindness to you?"

She smiled. "He did not declare himself to me, but you should know that would not dismay me. If he does not already love me, I am certain he will do so before long, and he will be glad I am here. You will see."

He was gazing at her curiously all the time she was speaking and after a moment asked, "What have you done to your hair?"

She chuckled. "I took some of Papa's wig powder to tone down the colour, should anyone seek to comment on the likeness between us. We are very much alike, Myles, and the colour of our hair very noticeable indeed. I have done it up in the latest style too. I dare say if Papa were to see me now he would fail to recognise me."

He shook his head. "You are quite incorrigible. What am I to do with you?"

She took up her gloves and hat, putting the latter on her head and tying the ribbons. "I must go now, dearest, before Evangeline arrives home from her portrait sitting."

"It seems there is nought I can do save allow you to continue on this mad course, otherwise I shall precipitate just the scandal I wish to avoid. You have placed me in an impossible position."

She chuckled and then kissed him on the cheek. "Precisely."

"However, there is one problem you are not aware of. . . ." She looked at him quizzically. "Lady Berriman is in Town."

She stiffened slightly as she pulled on her gloves. "Oh, really? I fancy it will make no odds to me."

"Miranda, she is our god-mother. She may well recognise you and it is foolish to think you will not meet."

"She will not recognise me. She has not seen me or concerned herself with my welfare—spiritual or otherwise—since Mama died."

"When I spoke to her only last week she did

mention she had been considering launching you into Society."

"Three years too late! I would be an old maid of fifty before she finally decided to do her duty."

Myles stroked his chin thoughtfully. "She did say you were always too boisterous to be ladylike and she was afraid you might be a bad influence on her own girls."

"Hah! Excuses. She is only afraid I will outshine her own friday-faced brood."

Myles chuckled. "I dare say that's true. She does push Constance at me at every opportunity. I wouldn't mind, only she is so much taller than I and giggles every time I address a remark to her."

They laughed for a few moments and then he added, "All the same, Miranda, if she does see you. . . ."

"I have changed in appearance since our last meeting which must be all of ten years ago, and she will not expect to see me as Evangeline Devilliars' companion. I believe I am safe from even her eagle eyes."

Her brother looked slightly mollified as he walked with her to the door. "I had better escort you back to Portman Square."

"Oh no. We may be seen together and it would not do." She smiled. "No doubt we shall meet at social gatherings before long. I assume that you do move in similar circles to the Dornfords."

"Quite often." He looked troubled again.

She paused to put one hand on his arm. "You really have no cause to worry on my account, Myles. In the one week I have spent in London I have enjoyed myself more than I can ever remember and Evangeline really is a dear. Apart from looking like an angel, she also possesses the sweetest nature. . . ."

Myles Templeton put up one hand to silence her. "Oh, please save me from such praise. 'Tis enough that Cornelius is forever singing her praises. . . ."

His voice tailed away into confusion as his sister's eyes grew bleak. "Cornelius? Is *he* one of Evangeline's admirers?" He tried to bluster but she insisted firmly, "Myles, I must *know*."

"Cornelius has called on her. Miranda," he entreated, "it is only because she is the toast of the town, the current rage of the *ton*. Even *I* have paid token court. . . ."

"Do *you* not admire her?"

"Oh, she is a pleasing enough chit, but she has an empty head. No, I cannot say I am taken with her and the same will be true of Cornelius."

She smiled again. "It is just as I expected, but once he is able to see me again it will be as before. You will see I am right."

He did not answer, but merely dashed into the street to hail a passing chair. As he helped her into it he said fiercely, "If you find life unbearable for any reason you will come here to me immediately."

She smiled. "Naturally, but I cannot imagine why life should suddenly become unbearable."

"I know Dornford better than you, dearest. He hasn't a very . . . savoury reputation with the ladies and if you are in a position of subordination he may be too free with you."

He closed the door and she leaned forward. "You need have no fear on that score. He has already informed me he has no taste for innocence."

The look of horror on her brother's face moved her to laugh merrily. He gripped onto the door whilst the chairmen waited patiently to be off. "When did he have cause to say this to you?"

"It is nothing for you to get in a pucker about, Myles. Lord Dornford is rarely in the house for me to see, and when he is I promise you he scarce speaks to me."

She indicated to the chairmen that she was ready to go and giving him an impish smile left her brother standing in the road scowling after her.

Chapter Five

The Haymarket Theatre was packed that night with all those who were of any consequence in Society. Miranda grew round-eyed seeing all the magnificent gowns, towering hairstyles and myriad jewels, but in her hand-me-down gown she felt as elegant as anyone there. Even though all her own jewellery—such as it was—remained at her home, Miranda had fashioned a necklet out of velvet which matched her gown and this was much admired, first by Evangeline and then by her aunt.

It was a brand new production of *The Beggar's Opera* which had attracted so great a turn-out, and it was being performed particularly well that evening and not one mischievous buck dared to throw rotten fruit onto the stage.

As the curtain came down on the first act Miranda turned excitedly to Evangeline, saying, "Isn't it magnificent?"

"It is tolerably good," she conceded, looking around to see how many of her admirers were present.

From the pit their box was receiving a great many appreciative glances so it was clear the young lady was not going to be disappointed. Lady Pendlebury who, much to Miranda's surprise, had dozed during the first act, got to her feet now.

"I believe I see the duchess over there in her box. I must have a coze with her. You girls can send Adams for lemonade if you require it."

With that she lumbered out of the box. Excitedly Miranda looked around the crowded auditorium but for quite a different reason from Evangeline. Suddenly she froze as her eyes came to rest on a lady sitting in an adjacent box who was viewing them through a quizzing glass. A few seconds later she knew who the person was—Lady Berriman, her godmother, accompanied by three of her plain daughters. Miranda put up her fan immediately and averted her face, saying to her companion, "The lady in the next box is quizzing us, Evangeline."

The girl looked to see who it was and then away again, displaying little interest. "Oh, that is Lady Berriman. She is of no account. No doubt she is wondering who you are."

When Miranda dared to glance at her again a few moments later she was relieved to discover she was no longer the object of Lady Berri-

man's interest and was able to study the lady
herself. Her gown and hair were of an exaggerated style, aping the current vogue for elabora-
tion to the point of vulgarity as did her three
daughters. She could not understand the link
of friendship which had existed between Lady
Berriman and her own sweet mama. It could
not have been such a great one on Lady Berriman's side for her to have ignored Miranda and
her brother so studiously for all of ten years.

She transferred her gaze away from Lady
Berriman's box when one of the girls became
aware of her scrutiny, but she gasped aloud
when she found herself looking instead directly at the marquis who was seated in a box facing theirs. He smiled slightly and inclined his
head to her. Miranda acknowledged him with a
slight inclination of her own head and then
transferred her attention to the lady at his
side.

Her appearance could only be described as
exquisite—in every way. She was very beautiful, with a white complexion and dark, lus-
trous eyes. Her hair was well-powdered and
done up in a confection of curls, feathers and
bows, and her elaborate gown, which revealed
a great deal of her snowy-white bosom, was of
the finest stuff.

Miranda turned to Evangeline. "The marquis is in the box facing ours. Did you know?"

His sister did not even trouble to look; she
was smiling to a buck in the pit. "Oh yes, that

is Isabella, Countess of Bascombe at his side, his *chère amie*."

Miranda was taken aback and stole another glance, but although the beautiful countess was there, the marquis was no longer to be seen. Evangeline smiled at her companion's surprise. "The elderly gentleman is the Earl of Bascombe, and he is exceedingly rich. They have a new house facing the Park." She giggled. "Isabella has blackamoors to serve her and a monkey for a pet too. She has a page who wears a diamond studded collar. Oh yes, and he has a liking for marchpane!"

"The blackamoor?"

"No, the monkey, you goose!"

Miranda glanced across to their box once again. "I notice the earl is considerably older than his wife, but does he not mind. . . .?"

Evangeline laughed. "It is quite a usual arrangement, you know. Dornford and Lady Bascombe are very devoted and have been for years. Lord Bascombe, I am sure, no longer cares; he is so old. His wife gave him a son within a year of the marriage which satisfied him well enough. The odd thing is, the silly fool is the only one who has not noticed how like the Dornfords the child is."

Miranda continued to look shocked which made the other girl laugh all the more. "You are so naive, Miranda. How old are you?"

"Twenty," she answered, hating to be

laughed at. It was something which rarely happened to her.

"I am only seventeen but I declare I am more knowledgeable than you." She leaned towards her. "Have you never had a *beau?*"

The thought of Cornelius warmed her but she answered, "There has never been a suitable opportunity."

"Poor you. But you are not ill-looking; perhaps whilst you are in Town. . . ."

Miranda looked across the auditorium once more. "Lady Bascombe is very beautiful."

"But no longer young. She must be almost thirty and it is rumoured she uses a prodigious number of paints on her skin and she buys Count Cagliostro's *Beautifying Water* and *Wine of Egypt.* One irons out wrinkles and the other . . ." she laughed, "keeps the spirit young."

Miranda laughed too. "I shall keep it in mind should I ever be in need."

Evangeline shuddered. "I would hate to be old. I cannot bear to think of it."

Thoughtfully Miranda asked, "Has the marquis known Lady Bascombe for a very long time?"

"Oh, for years. Before she was married to the earl."

"Did he not wish to marry her himself?"

"I believe so. She had so many admirers, it seems, but she only loved Dornford, so she used the earl's attachment to try and bring him up to scratch more quickly. Well, Dornford has an extraordinary amount of pride and it had quite the opposite effect. He left her to the earl and she had little choice but to marry him."

Evangeline grinned engagingly. "You may be sure I will not make the same mistake. My true love will be left in no doubt of the fact and I will accept no other as my husband."

Miranda replied, "And I should hope always to be true to my husband."

"*That* is quite demode." She smiled across at someone and then said, "There is dear Mr. Osborne and Mr. Templeton."

Miranda immediately followed the direction of Evangeline's gaze and her heart began to thump noisily at the sight of Cornelius. Dressed superbly, he looked as handsome as ever but the blue eyes she had, not long ago, gazed into rapturously bulged with disbelief and although she bowed and smiled he appeared rooted to the spot. Angrily she realised Myles had not yet told him of her presence in the Town and moments later the two young men could be seen in earnest conversation. She could guess much of what was being said.

"Do you know them?" she asked.

Evangeline looked suddenly bashful. "Oh yes," she answered with a sigh.

Miranda was still looking at her questioningly when the two young men were admitted to the box by Adams, the footman. Evangeline knew all the correct and clever responses to their questions and accepted the lemonade they had thoughtfully procured.

Miranda deemed it prudent to remain partially concealed behind her fan lest her adoring glances at Cornelius be seen by her friend, but at length Evangeline said, "Oh do allow me to introduce my dear friend to you. Mr. Templeton, Mr. Osborne, this is Miss Crawley."

Cornelius looked almost afraid of her as he acknowledged the introduction, stammering and stuttering which was out of character, but entirely endearing. "Do you enjoy your stay, Miss . . . er . . . Crawley?" he enquired.

Impishly she replied, "Most certainly. I have met so few people as yet so I am delighted to make *your* acquaintance, Mr. Osborne."

His cheeks turned slightly pink and Miranda fancied he was relieved when Evangeline claimed his attention once more. Myles then took the opportunity of moving closer to her.

"Clement weather for the time of the year?" he ventured in a strangled voice.

He looked so uncomfortable she felt like hugging him, but merely answered in a demure voice, "Exceedingly clement, Mr. Templeton. The performance is quite exceptional. I cannot wait to see the fate of MacHeath and poor Polly."

"It will end happily, you will see."

Glancing at Evangeline she saw her well-involved in conversation with Cornelius and from behind her fan whispered, "Lady Berriman is in the next box, Myles, and has been quizzing us all through this interval. Call in on her and see if she is suspicious."

He nodded. "If she is, all will be up, you understand. There will be a frightful row."

Miranda's spirits fell. "Let us hope she is unaware after all."

At that moment the marquis himself came into the box. He looked supremely elegant in bottle green coat which was fastened by diamond buttons and there were diamond buckles on his shoes too.

"Ah, I see you are well-taken care of," he said in a bright tone, "so I shall not linger."

The two young men, however, found it a good opportunity to take their leave and did so with alacrity. Miranda watched them go longingly but consoled herself with the thought they would meet often in the future.

"Where is Aunt Malzena?" he asked.

"With the duchess of Frensham, I believe. She will return before long."

A moment later Miranda felt his burning gaze upon her and when she was forced to look at him he said, "How do you enjoy the London theatre, Miss Crawley?"

"Exceedingly well, I thank you, Lord Dornford. And you?"

"I regret not on this occasion. I am here as Lord Bascombe's guest and the countess is unwell so we must leave immediately. I have sent

for her carriage and have just come to take my
leave of you. Good night, ladies."

The second act was about to begin and everyone was now returning to their seats. Lady
Pendlebury came back into the box and settled
into her seat in the corner.

Miranda could see that Lady Bascombe was
being helped from the box by her husband and
the marquis and murmured to Evangeline, "I
wonder what ails Lady Bascombe."

"She has been ailing for some time. It is
said," Evangeline added, "she paints her face
too much. Such an illness has been known to
happen before."

Myles and Cornelius Osborne had also taken
their seats once more. Miranda looked anxiously to her brother and to her great relief he
shook his head almost imperceptibly. Lady
Berriman had not recognised her. She glanced
at Lady Pendlebury whose chin was already
resting on her bosom and smiled to herself.

Evangeline was coyly fanning herself and
pretending the two young men did not exist
but after a few moments she could no longer
contain herself and leaned towards Miranda
conspiratorially.

"Do you not think Mr. Osborne is the hand-
somest man alive?"

Miranda was startled by the question, for at
that moment thoughts of Cornelius were milling in her own mind, but she managed to an-

swer quite truthfully, "He has the most pleasing countenance."

With deep foreboding she looked at the girl whose pink cheeks were partially hidden by her fan, but her eyes could clearly be seen and they sparkled brightly.

"Do you have a partiality towards him?" Miranda asked hesitantly, fearing to hear the answer.

"You are very astute, Miranda; you have guessed my secret, which must for now remain between the two of us. It is all so new to me and I cannot be certain he returns my feelings, although I am quite sure that he does. Oh, Miranda, I have never felt like this before, so it must be love."

Miranda was glad to be able to hide her look of dismay behind her fan which was just as well for Evangeline's next words disconcerted her further. "Mr. Templeton seemed to be quite taken by you," she said coyly. "You could do worse than encourage him. He is very well-connected, I am told."

She just could not answer and turned away to the stage where the second act was now under way. It was still new to her and as interesting as before but the excitement and magic of the evening was quite gone.

At home in Sussex time always passed with agonising slowness for Miranda who invariably found herself counting the days between

Myles's visits, but in London the time passed without her really being aware of it happening. Days and nights were filled with activity and as Evangeline had promised Miranda accompanied her to many balls, routs and parties. Some functions, such as evenings at Almacks, were so exclusive they were closed to Miranda, of course, but there were not many and usually she welcomed the respite except for fretting over a lost opportunity to see Cornelius, for she was discovering that being in London was no guarantee of seeing him. So many people attended the social affairs of the *ton* it was difficult at times to exchange more than a greeting, and to Miranda's growing dismay Evangeline used every feminine wile to attract his attention and keep him at her side.

Miranda did meet a great many people and was often asked to dance by fashionable young men, but she was sure this was more out of deference to Evangeline than any partiality towards her. Not that this troubled her; only one man was of interest and there were occasions when she was requested to dance by Cornelius—Myles too—which were pure heaven. She discovered that her heart's delight was glad to see her after all, but Evangeline was a formidable rival. Miranda could not hope to compete; she could not even use her own limited powers to keep him at her side. Fortunately, snug in her own happy dream, Evangeline did not notice her companion's growing frustration.

One of the regular occasions when Evangeline received attention from her admirers was during their morning ride in Hyde Park, not far from the Tyburn gibbet which had horrified her so on her arrival. Winter was almost over, gone, for once, with Miranda scarce noticing it—and the weather was pleasant for riding.

On one such day Miranda had the misfortune to come once again under the scrutiny of Lady Berriman who was also out riding with her daughter Constance in her landau. The carriage stopped by their party and the gentlemen present raised their hats but Miranda felt only panic as the imperious lady fixed her with a steely eye.

Fortunately Evangeline came to her rescue, saying, "Lady Berriman, I don't believe you have made Miss Crawley's acquaintance as yet. She is a friend who is at present staying with us at Dornford House."

Miranda felt the woman's gaze burning through her and the tension was becoming unbearable when she said at last, "No, I don't believe we are acquainted," and with a curt nod of her head went on her way.

Miranda drew a heartfelt sigh of relief and as they resumed their ride discovered Lord Dornford's eyes upon her which increased both the guilt and confusion she was feeling. Suddenly she was tempted to make a confession to him and beg Evangeline's forgiveness, but merely continued on her way with the others.

It was only occasionally that the marquis would join them, making an impressive sight on his coal black mare, and always at such times his sister would be excited, as if experiencing a special treat. Miranda and Myles had always been as close as only twins could be, but she was touched by the affection Evangeline had for her brother. She only deemed it a pity he did not reciprocate such feelings. On more than one occasion Miranda found herself wondering if he truly had affection for anyone —Lady Bascombe in particular—and the thought invariably made her shudder.

Despite all her earlier ambitions to enjoy every social activity in the Town, she found that her favourite occupation was riding in the Park; perhaps because here she need not pretend so hard and could relax a little. Also, out in the open amongst the trees and fields with their grazing herds, she was more at home, for it was in the country she had spent the first twenty years of her life. Riding in the Park bore no relation, however, to country gallops. It was altogether a more civilised affair, with pathways crowded by not only horses and their riders, but pedestrians and carriages too, so it was not possible to do more than canter— and rarely that.

Dressed in a bottle green habit and riding a

chestnut mare, Evangeline was always the centre of attention, surrounded by adoring *beaux* who laid in wait for her to appear and then pretended it was mere coincidence. Despite the number of them, the girl still seemed to favour Cornelius, so much so that comment was at last beginning to be made.

Miranda had expected Evangeline's ardour to pall before long, but when this did not happen she began to despair. She saw that she was losing him in the very way she had dreaded. It was what had prompted her flight from home, but she was beginning to realise nothing could be worse than having to stand by and watch it happen. That she was so fond of Evangeline too made it all harder to bear.

"Myles," she said to her brother as they rode along the crowded path one sunny morning, "I'm persuaded Evangeline is in love with Cornelius."

"He is a lucky fellow to be so much in demand," he answered brightly, but his smile faded at her agonised look.

She glanced behind to see Evangeline surrounded as usual by a host of admirers but with Cornelius in pride of place at her side. On this occasion her brother rode at her other side and what a handsome trio they made.

A moment later Miranda returned her attention to her brother. "You do not seem to comprehend my dilemma, Myles. I have come here so that Cornelius and I can see each other."

"And so you do."

"We are fortunate if we have the opportunity to pass the time of day."

"Cornelius cannot do more. He has expressed his wish to me to be more in *your* company but it is impossible without arousing suspicion, and you are the one who wishes most of all to avoid that." He chuckled. "We are so often thrown together I am surprised there is no gossip about *us*."

For the moment her good humour was restored and she smiled. "At the theatre Evangeline did venture to say there might be possibilities. Is that not famous?"

She glanced behind and Evangeline smiled encouragingly at her and Miranda looked quickly away again. It was at this point that an elegant phaeton slowed down at their side. Miranda's attention was immediately diverted by the lady sitting beside an elegant young buck who was tooling the ribbons, for it was none other than Lady Bascombe. Miranda had not so far seen her at such close quarters, for she attended so few social occasions, and as the gentlemen politely raised their hats and the lady inclined her head in acknowledgement Miranda noticed the paleness of her complexion, the redness of her lips, and wondered if perhaps Evangeline was after all correct about the amount of paint she used. If so, it was cer-

tainly to good effect; there could be no other
woman to compare with her looks in the entire
Town. Today she was wearing a pale pink polonaise gown and pinafore with a milkmaid's hat
on her high-piled curls, and even Evangeline's
prettiness faded by comparison to this gorgeous creature. She could well understand the
marquis's devotion and knew he must regret
the lost chance of being her husband. It was no
wonder he was so cynical about marriage; it
must be, Miranda thought pityingly, a purgatory he would have to live through every day.

She stole a glance at the marquis but he remained impassively by his sister's side until
the phaeton passed on and they could resume
their ride, which was often interrupted by such
encounters, although not all were of so much
interest to Miranda.

Urging her mare forward she said in a low
voice to Myles, "Have you heard the rumours
about Lady Bascombe and Lord Dornford?"

"Oh, 'tis not rumour; the liason is a long-
standing one, and no longer invites comment."

She was surprised and more than a little disappointed, for she had hoped, for some reason
she could not identify, that it was not after all
true. After a moment or too she put the marquis's *amours* from her mind and plucked up
enough courage to ask, "Does Cornelius intend
to offer for Evangeline?"

Myles looked at her in some surprise. "I
don't know. He has not mentioned the matter

to me so I am sure it cannot be imminent. He would not, I fancy, in any event have a chance. Dornford would not consider a mere common-er as husband for his sister, well-placed as Cornelius happens to be. Lady Evangeline is too well-endowed. There are too many titles in pursuit of her."

"That may be true. Several have already de-clared themselves but Evangeline herself told me that her brother will allow her to follow her heart in this matter and she fully intends to do so."

"He is less of a tyrant than I imagined."

"Oh, he is simply not interested," Miranda answered irritably. "He has made it clear he expects her to marry by the end of this season and that is merely so he can be free to pursue his own interests. To whom Evangeline is mar-ried does not concern him overmuch although I assume he would not countenance an out and out misalliance. But there is little chance of that. As you can see Evangeline has quite a choice even though," she added despondently, "it appears she has already made it."

"Tomorrow may be quite a different matter. Lady Evangeline is known to be capricious in her affections."

"I have been thinking so for weeks, but Cornelius remains firmly her favourite. Won't it be the greatest irony, Myles, if I re-turn home to Papa after seeing Evangeline wed to Cornelius?"

He raised his hat to a group of people strolling past and they in turn acknowledged his greeting. "What can I do to help?" he asked, gazing at her sympathetically. "I promise you Corny isn't as enamoured of her."

"I must be forgiven for thinking so."

"It appears you will just have to be patient."

"I cannot bear it any longer. You have no notion how it is, being Evangeline's confidante. It's far worse than watching from a distance."

"Dare I suggest you leave the marquis's service?" he asked slyly and she shot him an angry look.

"I do not give in so easily."

He sighed. "That is what I feared. Perhaps I should go and snatch her from under Corny's nose."

"What a splendid idea!" she exclaimed, almost under her breath. "I can think of no better course save for you to take his place." His face creased into a frown and she went on excitedly. "I know you were only jesting, but think on it; you are handsome and the heir to a baronetcy. You have every qualification to become the favourite. If you can distract her from Cornelius just a little . . . don't you see, Myles. . . .?"

He laughed. "Oh, I quite see. You would have me join that company of moonfaces? Oh no, Miranda, you must be roasting me."

Miranda did not echo his amusement. "It is

not a joke. You have enough charm to turn any girl's head when you choose to do so. I have seen you do it so now put it to good use."

"Do you mean me to tell her she has hair softer than the finest silk, eyes brighter than the most precious jewel?"

"Yes, yes, exactly. That is precisely what I do mean."

"Would you be moved by such declarations?"

"Not I, but I promise you Evangeline puts much store by such compliments."

He laughed. "Oh, I cannot. What if she believes I'm in earnest?"

"Once you begin to cry off another favourite will soon take your place and in the meanwhile, hopefully, I will have Cornelius's attention again."

"It wouldn't work."

She gazed at him piteously. "If not, I shall be at no further disadvantage than now. Please try, Myles, I beg of you. It was your idea after all."

"Yes, and I'd as lief cut out my tongue than say anything to you again."

She laughed and he drew a deep sigh. "My mind is filled with foreboding."

She glanced behind to discover the marquis was staring at them both and although his face was expressionless, it did wear a slight frown. As their eyes met Miranda started guiltily and looked away again. When she dared to look again to her alarm he was moving slowly towards her.

"Dornford is coming," she said in a frantic whisper. "This is your chance. Drop back, Myles, and attend to Evangeline closely. You have far more address than Cornelius, you know."

He looked startled but had no chance to reply before Lord Dornford's mount came between them. "It is a fine day, is it not?" he said in a bright voice, inhaling the air deeply.

Miranda smiled with uncertainty, for his presence invariably made her feel uncomfortable, she had discovered. It was, she thought, the memory of the night they had spent together at the inn. To give him his due he had never sought to remind her of it since, yet she knew he would not forget, no more than she.

"It is indeed, Lord Dornford, and the herald of even better things to come."

She flashed a meaningful glance at her brother who, looking rather regretful, dropped back and a moment later, to Miranda's satisfaction had managed to manoevre his mount into position at Lady Evangeline's side. Lord Dornford noticed it too, but did not comment. As the horses picked their way along carefully Miranda found it impossible to find anything to say to him. As her employer it was necessary for her to treat him with the utmost respect, something she found difficult to do. He would not forget the insults she had hurled at him no more than she.

"You seem to find Mr. Templeton agreeable company," he murmured some moments later.

Miranda laughed hollowly. "He understands how bewildering it is for me, knowing so few people."

"It is good of him to be kind to you."

"So many others too," she assured him.

"Then your stay is an enjoyable one."

"I must admit it is. My situation can hardly be considered an onerous one, although that is due in great part to the sweet nature of Lady Evangeline."

"You make me see her in an entirely different light," he answered and Miranda's fingers tightened around her whip.

She would have liked to have used it on him, telling him, "Evangeline adores you." Fortunately she also knew that the girl was totally unaware of her brother's disinterest in her. She, no doubt, imagined he adored her in much the same way.

"The town has not disappointed you, I presume?"

"Indeed not," she answered heartily, "except of course," she added in a more subdued voice, "there does seem to be a great deal of poverty which I find distressing."

"But only because it is not hid from sight. The poor in London come amongst us and do not huddle in some country hovel where they cannot be seen."

"I have never seen such hovels as you describe, Lord Dornford." She looked at him boldly which did not dismay him and then quickly away again. "At least not on my . . . Sir Geoffrey Trimm's estate."

"And not I assure you on any of mine, Miss Crawley.

"I have noticed," he went on a moment later, "that you ride exceptionally well."

"You flatter me, Lord Dornford. In the country where I have, you will recall, spent most of my life, riding is more of a necessity than a pleasure."

"Riding as we are doing now must become onerous."

"Not at all. I enjoy it."

He looked at her curiously. "Would you not like to give your horse its head?"

"It would be well nigh impossible on these paths without killing someone in the process, myself also I fear and I have a strong sense of self preservation."

"I had noticed," he answered dryly, but when she shot him a sharp look his expression was a bland one. "I did mean across the fields. Shall we indulge ourselves, Miss Crawley?"

She glanced behind and could not help but smile at the sight of Evangeline attending every word uttered by Myles, although she could not hear what they were saying. Her

brother, she had long been aware, had no notion of the effect he could have on ladies both
young and old.

Before she could answer the marquis he said,
smiling ironically, "You need have no fear for
my sister. She is well-occupied and likely to be
for as long as she chooses to remain here. If I
recall correctly in the nursery I learned a
rhyme; *My face is my fortune, sir, she said.*"

Miranda made a gesture of irritation. "Although I would hesitate to contradict a man of
your standing, I believe with Evangeline she
possesses far more than a fair face. Her true
worth is in the sweetness of her nature."

Still smiling he answered, "Your loyalty is
heartwarming. Come, let us put these admirable beasts through their paces," he said, bring-
ing his whip down on her mare's flank.

The beast lunged forward, across the fields,
the wind tearing at her hat. A poor horse-
woman would have been unseated but Miranda was equal to it, although she was aware
that he could easily outride her and did. There
were moments though when she almost caught
up with him.

Chapter Six

There were times during the ensuing week that Miranda reflected her plan to free Cornelius from Evangeline's spell was working all too well. Myles was scarcely ever far from the girl's side.

A few days after her ride with Lord Dornford, a rout was held at Dornford House and promised to be a glittering occasion with everyone of any consequence attending. It wasn't necessary to have an excuse to hold a celebration of this kind but this particular one was being held on the pretext of displaying George Romney's portrait of Lady Evangeline. It was now complete and hung in the main drawing room replacing a dingy Dobson of some Dornford ancestor. The general consensus of opinion allowed that the likeness was a good one. Miranda considered the portrait of Evangeline, in her favourite blue lustring gown, captured the girl's fragile beauty perfectly.

That night Portman Square was choked with carriages of every type and the house itself was a blaze of candlelight. Music drifted from the ground floor windows into the street and the ballroom was a shifting tapestry of dancers. Apart from the main drawing room which had been set aside for the sumptuous buffet the smaller reception rooms were being used by those who preferred to gamble, and there were a great many of those. Lady Pendlebury was of course one such person and it was no wonder her nephew did not complain, for he himself did not move from the faro table until supper was announced.

Surrounded by a crowd of young people Evangeline inevitably held court in the supper room just as she had in the ballroom earlier, and Miranda was delighted to see no sign of Cornelius in that particular group although Myles had been close to her all evening. He really was a dear, she mused, for he had not complained once about the task she had set him and appeared to be making the best of it.

Miranda was approaching the supper table when a familiar voice said, "Miss Crawley, may I fetch you some supper?"

When she turned she found herself looking into the smiling face of Cornelius Osborne. Her heart fluttered unevenly but she managed to say in a calm voice, "Mr. Osborne, how kind of you."

Some few minutes later he had procured

some supper for her and found seats in a quiet corner where they could talk in reasonable privacy.

"You have no notion how difficult it has been for me," he said immediately, "knowing you to be so close and yet unable to see you or speak to you above a minute."

"I did not perceive a broken heart," she countered.

"If you are referring to my friendship with Lady Evangeline, she took a fancy to me and I could not snub her even if I wished to. And I couldn't take too much heed of *you*. Myles told me the entire story of which, incidentally, I do not approve." He glanced across to where Evangeline was laughing at something Myles had said. "Now it seems," he added a little bleakly, "Myles has taken her fancy. She is a capricious creature."

"Does it matter to you overmuch?" she asked in a gentle voice.

In truth he seemed more of a boy and much less of a man than he had during that idyllic summer, and the discovery startled her. She had risked so much to be at his side and although she did not regret doing so she did wonder if it had all been worth while.

"I do not mind at all now that you are here." He smiled suddenly and his face lighted up into the handsome countenance she had dreamed of so long. "I thought of you so much but did not believe I would see you again so soon."

"Then Lady Evangeline really did not mean . . . a great deal to you?" she asked hesitantly.

"She was here and you were not." His smile vanished. "This masquerade is deuced awkward, Miranda. How can we possibly meet?"

"We will contrive to arrange something. It will be easier now Evangeline does not require your attention."

He laughed. "That is indeed a consolation."

Many of the guests were wandering back into the ballroom and the music was starting up again. Miranda felt a stab of apprehension when she caught sight of Lord Dornford in conversation with some of his acquaintances. He was head and shoulders taller than any of them, she noted, and although he was not as handsome as Cornelius he was a far more imposing man.

"Are you engaged for this next set?" Cornelius was asking.

At that moment she found herself once more being quizzed by Lady Berriman from across the room and she averted her face quickly. How she feared that woman's presence. She was a constant threat and reminder of the peril of her situation.

"Miranda," Cornelius insisted, "I would like to stand up for this set with you."

She returned her attention to him at last. "I

am sorry. My god-mother is over there, quizzing me, and I am quite alarmed by it."

He looked aghast. "Hasn't she recognised you yet?"

"She hasn't seen me since I was ten years old so she couldn't possibly recognise me now. My hair is normally like a beacon, but I keep it well powdered and none could possibly guess who I am. She is only curious as to my status in this house, but that in itself alarms me. Oh, here comes Viscount Lowe," she said as the elderly gentleman approached. "He has engaged me for this set." As she got to her feet she put one hand on Cornelius's arm. "Meet me after this set in the shrubbery. We will be undisturbed there."

From the fragmented shrieks and cries of laughter, Miranda discovered that the garden was not deserted after all. Others were about for reasons much the same as her own. There were a few lamps and lanterns about so she could easily see her way but after the warmth of the drawing rooms it was cold outside.

She walked slowly along the paths, wondering where Cornelius could be. A giggle from behind a tree made her start uneasily, but then she moved on.

"Cornelius," she whispered hesitantly as the lights and noise from the house faded into the distance. "Cornelius, are you there?"

She was answered by a rustling sound and

then a few moments later he appeared on the path some yards away.

"Miranda, I am here." She hurried towards him gladly. "I thought you'd forgotten and was getting cold."

"The set was a long one and I did want to be sure of slipping away unseen."

He drew her away from the path, beneath an arbour which would soon begin to flower. "I have waited a long time for this," she told him, looking into his face. "I came to London expressly to be near you, but I had no notion how difficult that was going to be. At home I didn't appreciate the ease with which we could meet and converse."

He put his arms around her and she relaxed against his shoulder. "I'm unhappy about this ruse, but I cannot help but be glad you are here. You are a grand spirited girl. There can be few like you. You're like a rare jewel, flawless and perfect."

She smiled up at him. "I dislike the pretence and the subterfuge even more than you, but there was no other way, and it is perhaps better than I had planned. I console myself that no one will be hurt by it."

He held her tighter, saying, "When I left your home at the beginning of this Season I only regretted that I did not beg permission to kiss you before I went."

Her heart fluttered unevenly. "You may ask now."

He bent to kiss her heartily and when at last he drew away breathless, she was left rather bemused. She had expected more from what she had been told of such matters. It was her first kiss but she felt no different after it.

As she mused on it his arms went rigid around her. "Someone is coming along this path," he said in alarm.

"There are many people out here tonight," she murmured.

"Only listen, Miranda, the footsteps are not those of lovers; they are heavy ones, deliberately coming this way." He looked down on her. "Stay quietly with me. We are well concealed."

"I hope you may be right," she answered in a whisper. "If anyone should report to the marquis that his sister's companion had an assignation in the shrubbery I would suffer his considerable wrath, and deservedly."

"Never fear. In such a case I will declare myself."

Miranda was no longer moved by such an offer and replied, "Myles would not thank you for that, Cornelius. The gossip would make him furious and I dare not think what the marquis would say to learn he had been hoaxed."

Cornelius squeezed her arm and they lapsed into an uneasy silence and for the next few moments all that could be heard was the beating of their own hearts and the occasional footsteps on the gravel.

"Miss Crawley, are you there?"

Miranda caught her breath and Cornelius said, "That's torn it! It's Lord Dornford himself. Why is he looking for you?"

"I don't know. He must have seen me leave," she said in a vexed whisper. "That man has eyes like a cat. Sometimes I think he has supernatural powers." She put one hand up to her hair and made sure it was not dishevelled. "Stay concealed," she told Cornelius. "I will draw his attention and we may yet avoid embarrassment."

Before he had any opportunity to object Miranda walked back to the path to find Lord Dornford standing some yards away from where she had been concealed.

"Did I hear you call for me, Lord Dornford," she said demurely, although in truth her heart was beating painfully.

He turned on his heel just as she began to walk towards him and away from Cornelius. His eyes narrowed slightly as he stared at her. "I thought for a moment I must have been mistaken when I believed you out here."

She looked at him blankly. "I needed some air."

"That is understandable, but you have been out here for some time." He put the back of his hand on her cheek. "You are quite cold, Miss Crawley, and we cannot have you catching a chill. They have been known to be fatal."

"Your concern overwhelms me," she answered, suddenly breathless at the touch of his hand, "but I am quite robust."

She began to walk towards the house, Lord Dornford doggedly at her side, and she dared not look back.

"The rout is a great success," she ventured.

"I'm glad you deem it so."

She stole a glance at him but his expression was still bland. It was becoming quite frustrating never knowing his true thoughts, but she did hate his finding her in the garden in such humiliating circumstances, even if he did not know what those circumstances were. As they reached the terrace she had the awful suspicion he did know she'd had an assignation and vowed to herself that it would never happen again. In the future she would meet Cornelius only in the normal way, or not at all.

As Miranda had surmised, the defection of Cornelius Osborne's attention did not trouble Evangeline in the least. In fact she began to realise it was Evangeline herself who had a change of heart, which satisfied Miranda greatly and prevented her conscience from pricking. Much to her relief Evangeline was in the greatest of spirits as she could see the morning after the rout.

Lady Pendlebury had joined them for breakfast although she looked heavy-eyed and complained loudly from time to time that she had played too deep and that Lady Cummings was a slippery character.

Miranda and Evangeline grinned at each other as the old lady poured yet more coffee for herself and Evangeline whispered, "I fear Aunt Malzena consumed too much champagne last night."

Lady Pendlebury pushed back her chair, holding one hand to her head. "I knew I should not have risen before noon," she murmured. "I must adjourn to my room. Ackworthy can make me one of her tisanes which will soon put my digestion to rights."

Evangeline stifled a giggle behind her hand. "I sincerely hope so, Aunt Malzena. It would be sad indeed if you were to miss the duchess's card party this evening."

The old lady shot her niece a dark look. "I suspect you are being facetious, and I'll not have it."

"Oh no, Aunt Malzena! No indeed."

As she left the room, Evangeline could not longer stifle her laughter, and Miranda, although vastly amused too, scolded, "Shame on you. She is suffering greatly."

"Pay no heed to me. Whatever I may say to tease her, in truth I am exceedingly fond of my aunt, even though Dornford is her favourite."

"Talking of Lord Dornford, I am persuaded he has sensibly remained in his bed this morning," Miranda said carefully after a moment, still mindful of the minuet he had insisted they stand up for immediately after returning to the ballroom.

Afterwards he had introduced her to a group of people and in one way and another she had been kept so busy for the remainder of the evening she had not been able to exchange another word with Cornelius who after a while grew weary of waiting and moved on to one of the card rooms. Miranda had later learned that he had played too deep and was obliged to write a voucher for his losses.

"Not James," his sister answered. "I passed him on my way down this morning. He had already breakfasted and was on his way out. I declare I don't know how he manages it."

Miranda thought it even more remarkable how he had contrived to overtake the stage-coach and be at the "Fleece Inn" before her. There were times when she considered him superhuman and it was now clear his sister also questioned his abilities.

Evangeline clasped her hands around her cup. "I believe he has gone to visit Lady Bascombe. She didn't arrive last night so it is possible she is ailing again."

"The *Wine of Egypt* obviously has not had any effect," Miranda commented.

"But it has," Evangeline argued. "She looks much younger than her years."

"I was only funning, and perhaps I should not if the lady is truly ill, only there are so many who take to a daybed to become Interesting Invalids."

The other girl frowned. "There have been occasions in the past when I have wondered that myself, but I do recall peering through the bannister many a time to see her standing up for every dance. I recall a time when she was very active."

"Then I truly pity her. Does she not have a physician in attendance?"

"There have been many. Lord Bascombe has spared no expense; they have travelled to continental spas to seek relief for her and on one occasion Dornford rode to Bath to bring one doctor back here to see her."

Miranda was shocked. "And can none of them cure her?"

"I have heard, although I cannot put much credence upon it, that she has been told her paints and powders are slowly poisoning her skin, but Lady Bascombe says her skin is perfect and she would rather die than go unpainted."

Miranda was awe-struck for a few moments and then became aware that Evangeline was toying thoughtfully with her bread and butter. "What shall we do this morning?" she asked in a bright tone of voice to counter the rather sombre subject of their conversation.

Immediately she brightened. "I need some ribbons for my mask. You must recall there is to be a masked ball at Vauxhall Gardens next week and I am not prepared."

Miranda smiled. "Never fear. You must decide upon a design and I shall sew the mask for you. I need ribbons for mine too."

"There is a favourite shop of mine in St. James's Street," she mused. "I fancy we shall find just what we require there."

As Miranda gazed into her bright face for a few moments realisation slowly dawned. "St. James's Street? Doesn't Mr. Templeton lodge nearby?"

The girl considered for a moment and then answered lightly, "I do believe you are right, Miranda."

As Evangeline carefully tied the ribbons of her plumed hat she said to Miranda who was drawing on her gloves, "You have always seemed well-disposed towards Mr. Templeton."

She was for the moment taken aback by this piece of astuteness from Evangeline and then she answered, "He has always been amicably disposed towards me. I suppose that is because I'm a stranger and he is kind hearted."

Evangeline adjusted her hat in the ormolu mirror, tilting it to a rakish angle. "Do you not consider him . . . well-favoured?"

"Extremely."

"And his mode of address pleasing?"

"Very much so."

She dare not look at the girl for fear of giving

away her agitation. Suddenly Evangeline stamped her foot hard on the floor. "Miranda, you are being extremely provoking."

"I cannot think why."

"Are you or are you not . . ." she lowered her eyes, "affectionately disposed towards Myles Templeton?"

"So that is what you are trying to discover," she answered with a laugh. "Forgive me for mistaking you. I am not in love with him." Evangeline stared at her and she added, "How dare I presume to be?"

The girl continued to stare at her, much to Miranda's discomfiture. "One cannot help one's affections. It isn't always possible to fall in love where one chooses."

Miranda smiled. "Very true, but I am being perfectly honest with you. Now, may we be on our way?"

She walked towards the door which was immediately opened by a footman. Evangeline hurried after her and as they paused on the footpath where the carriage awaited them the girl said, "I apologise, Miranda; I did not mean to be a cross-patch."

"I did not consider you one—truly. I merely cannot always understand such round-about questions, but no doubt I shall soon learn."

The lackey was holding open the carriage door for them and with a sweet smile of conciliation Miranda was about to follow Evangeline into the laudalet when a horrendous cry rent the air. Both girls stopped to look, Miranda stiffening with indignation at the sight of a boy sweep, no more than eight years old, being soundly beaten by his master on the pavement a few yards away.

The boy screamed and struggled but the sweep showed him no mercy. After hesitating a moment, hoping that the dreadful assault would stop, Miranda strode towards them.

"Unhand that child!" she demanded, and to her surprise he did stop beating him although the child did not stop howling. He fell down on to the ground and continued to roll around in agony. "What is the meaning of this outrage?"

"Refuses to climb, he does, but 'ave no fear 'e'll go up the nob's chimney even if I 'ave to light the fire under 'im."

Indignantly she said, "I'm not at all surprised he refused. He's probably terrified and half-starved too by the look of him."

At this point the child made a bid to escape but the sweep caught him again and began to beat him once more.

"Stop it, I say!" she cried, and again he did so. "This is inhuman."

The sweep, a dirty fellow, was fast losing patience with her now. "Now, look 'ere, lady. . . ."

"I am looking and abhor what I see."

"This lad's m'own property, see, and I'll do with 'im 'ow I want."

He began to advance menacingly upon Miranda who glanced behind to see that both the coachman and the footman were alert, although this did not reassure her overmuch.

Evangeline was standing by the coach, biting her lip in apprehension. "Oh, do come, Miranda," she pleaded.

A moment later she gave out a squeal and Miranda looked round to see none other than the marquis striding round the corner into the square. He checked mid-stride when he saw the little group gathered near his house and the passers-by who had also paused to watch with interest this exchange between the sweep and the lady. Such entertainment was rarely to be had.

"What is happening?" the marquis demanded, looking from Miranda to his sister and then back again.

Miranda looked at him beseechingly. "Lord Dornford, you must do something! Please tell this fellow to stop beating this child."

"This 'ere's m'own property, yer lordship."

The marquis looked to Miranda again, saying irritably, "I cannot see what I can do. The fellow is in the right of it."

"There must be something! Just look at the boy. Half-starved, filthy, wearing nothing more than a few pitiful rags, and just look at his legs, Lord Dornford. They're red-raw; burned I shouldn't wonder."

The child sensing sympathy took the opportunity of howling once more, whereupon the marquis said in a disdainful voice, "Cease that noise or I shall beat you too." The boy obliged and he turned with the utmost patience to Miranda once more. "How else can we have our chimneys cleaned if not by someone small enough to climb up them? And no doubt the creature deserved to have his ears boxed."

"That 'e did," the sweep agreed.

"This went beyond boxed ears," Miranda stubbornly insisted. "Had he been allowed to continue, the boy would have been killed."

During this heated exchange the unfortunate boy was gazing at them all wide-eyed and uncomprehending. All of a sudden the sweep said, "I'm orf," and picking up his brushes began to move away, pulling the boy, who had begun to struggle anew, with him. He managed to go only a few steps before the marquis put out his cane to stop him.

"Not so fast, my man. You will stay put until the matter is resolved." He looked to Miranda again. "Well, Miss Crawley, what would have you me do? The boy belongs to the sweep. I cannot dispute it."

"If it is indeed true this human being belongs to this person," she shot him a venomous look, "then *I* wish to buy him. I shall make it worth his while to part with the child."

Lord Dornford gave her an astonished look. "Miss Crawley, you are roasting me!"

"I assure you I am not. Furthermore I have the means by which to do it. If you would be so kind as to loan me the money, I shall not be in your debt for long."

"I shall have to take your word for that."

"You have it, Lord Dornford."

For a moment she was afraid he would insist on knowing from what source the money was to be obtained and he was still looking at her increduously when the sweep said, "This lady's fit for Bedlam, yer lordship," and began to move away yet again.

"Stay where you are!" the marquis commanded and so authoritative was the order, he did so. Addressing Miranda once more he said, "Miss Crawley, I am inclined to agree with this fellow's assessment of your sanity, but you are so obviously in earnest. If you were so foolhardy as to purchase this boy, providing I were willing to persuade the sweep to let him go, what would you do with him?"

"Care for his wounds initially and see that he is fed and restored to health."

His eyebrows rose a fraction. "How do you intend to achieve this miracle? You have no place of your own."

"Lord Dornford," she said firmly, at the same time studiously avoiding his gaze, "last night at your home sufficient food was thrown away to keep every sweep's boy in London well fed for a month, and as for accommodation, you have many unused attics."

"But it is *you* who wishes to buy and care for

this . . ." he glanced at him with distaste,
". . . creature."

Suddenly Miranda's eyes filled with tears
and her voice was choked as she said, "Please,
Lord Dornford, I beg of you help me save this
child. I could not sleep soundly knowing it will
go ill with him."

Evangeline came forward then, saying, "He
is such a pathetic sight, James. I am in agreement with Miranda. He has been ill-treated
over a long period."

The marquis drew a deep sigh of resignation.
"Oh, very well, but I too must be considered a
candidate for Bedlam!" He turned on his heel.
"How much will you take for the boy?"

An avaricious gleam had appeared in the
sweep's eyes. He began to stroke his chin
thoughtfully, silently musing that the peccadi-
los of the Quality could be turned to good account. "Cost me dear, 'e did."

The marquis gave him a look of disdain.
"Most probably he was snatched from the
street. You will have no trouble in replacing
him in the same way. Ten guineas is what I'll
pay and not a penny more."

The marquis took out the coins and after a
moment's hesitation the sweep took them,
realising, no doubt, that he would truly receive
no more.

"'ere, 'e's yours," he said, pushing the bewildered boy onto the marquis. "Never was any
good. More trouble than 'e's worth, you'll see."

"Be gone with you," the marquis replied, "and don't let me see you around here again."

Seconds later the fellow was gone leaving Lord Dornford clutching at the child's ear. After a moment or two he let it go, staring down at his own soot-ladened hand in distaste.

As he took out his handkerchief Miranda gazed at him in admiration, but it was Evangeline who said, "Oh, that was brave of you, Miranda. I would not have dared."

"Praise be for that," her brother murmured, removing the last speck of soot from his hand.

"Lord Dornford," Miranda began.

When he looked at her her voice died away. "Miss Crawley, do you know what you have done?" When she didn't answer he went on, "The heir to the Dornford title and lands is a cousin of mine who at present resides in the country—out of necessity rather than choice. If he was to learn to this morning's folly he is like to have me confined to an asylum and claim his birthright."

At this moment the ragamuffin decided to chance his luck and run, but the marquis was too fast for him. He caught him fast and was rewarded by a farrago of the most foul language it had ever been Miranda's misfortune to hear. Both girls gasped and their cheeks grew red whilst the marquis's face became dark with anger.

In disgust he pushed him towards the footman. "Have this creature made clean and see that his mouth is included in the scrubbing."

The footman caught the child, saying, "Certainly, my lord. Sounds as if his mother fed him with a fire shovel when he was young."

Miranda tried once more to voice her apologies to the marquis but he turned on his heel and quickly strode down the street.

She looked at Evangeline then, saying, "I *am* sorry, Evangeline."

"You are quite right to do what you did. I am so glad you saved him further suffering."

Miranda gave her a wan smile. "You must reserve your thanks for Lord Dornford. Without his assistance all would have been lost and I fear he is right; it is madness. One child is rescued from purgatory but there must be thousands like him and we cannot hope to help *them*."

Evangeline became quite melancholy at the thought and then brightened. "When I am a married lady with an establishment of my own, I will form a movement to help the children, just like the Foundling Hospital was created to help orphans."

Miranda squeezed her hand encouragingly and then together they went back into the house to see what could be done with the child.

Chapter Seven

It took four of them to bathe him. A sheet had
been spread in front of the hurriedly kindled
fire in Miranda's room and the bath had been
brought out and filled with hot water. But the
boy did not fancy having his rags torn off by
women, nor having to suffer their ministra-
tions in any way.

Miranda had hoped to coax him into co-op-
eration but despite his poor emaciated body he
had a surprising strength and resisted with all
his might, and at last she and Evangeline, and
the maidservant who had stayed to help, had
to call in a footman. Only then did they manage to strip and bathe him. Once he was clean
they were all horrified at the burns and bruises
on his body and the frequent paroxyms of
coughing which racked his little body. Evangeline was near to tears at the sight of him.

"What is your name?" Miranda asked when
he was at last clean and wrapped in a warm
bath towel. As he was about to answer she

135

added, "And we want none of your gutter
language. It will not be tolerated in this
household."

"Luke," he answered sullenly.

"Where are your mother and father, Luke?"

"Got none."

"Don't you remember either of them?"

"Never 'ad any."

"How old are you?"

"Dunno, and I dunno what you want me
for."

"Nothing, Luke. We just want to make life a
little easier for you and find work more congenial to you."

"Can find me own work," he coughed. "Got
nimble fingers, I 'ave. Pick the pocket of any
gentry cove, I can."

Miranda was horrified even though Evangeline had to stifle a giggle. "You mustn't. It's
wrong and if you're caught you will be put into
prison, or worse."

"Goin' on the gibbet's better'n going up the
chimney."

"You will never do *that* again," Miranda
vowed in a voice husky with emotion.

At this point Lady Pendlebury came burst-
ing into the room, fixing Miranda with an ac-
cusing eye. "What is all the . . . oh, who *is*
this?"

With words spilling over themselves
Evangeline began to explain and as she did so
her aunt's eyes grew wider. "Lord preserve us,"

she uttered at last. "Do you mean James actually aided and abetted this folly?"

"Oh, Aunt Malzena," Evangeline gasped, clasping her hands together, "you should have seen Miranda stand up to that vile creature, and Dornford too. She was magnificent."

"I would like to have seen it, to be sure."

"Lady Pendlebury," Miranda broke in, "could you possibly find a night shirt for him whilst I anoint his burns. I have some balm which should do, but have no idea how to go about clothing him."

The old lady stroked her chin thoughtfully. "One of Dornford's ordinary shirts might do. I'll send a footman along with it and I know where I can find some day clothes for him. I'd better have some good beef broth sent up too. By the looks of him, he needs it."

"Oh, thank you, Lady Pendlebury."

She merely sniffed as she went out, murmuring, "I hope we may be safe in our beds."

When the boy was dressed in one of Lord Dornford's shirts, which was more than big enough to serve as a night shirt, Miranda had another struggle to anoint the burns with balm and the footman was again called in to help. When the child spit at him the lackey hit back.

"Please don't strike him," Miranda begged. "He is so accustomed to ill-treatment he cannot understand we mean him no harm."

"Sorry, ma'am," the man muttered.

"Luke," she said firmly, "we are all trying to help you. Why do you fight us?"

"Dunno."

"Allow us to be kind to you. It will be much easier, I promise you."

After that she was allowed to anoint his burns with balm and the aid of the footman was no longer required. Even though Miranda strove to be gentle she knew she had hurt him. The fact that he was so obviously accustomed to pain smote at her heart.

When he was at last tucked up into the truckle bed she'd had erected in her own room, she spoon fed him with the beef broth and before it was half finished he could no longer fight fatigue and fell fast asleep. Miranda drew a deep sigh of relief and straightened up, smiling at Evangeline who had soot marks all over her gown and down her face. Miranda knew she too must look as dishevelled although she had been provident in borrowing one of the housekeeper's aprons and covered her hair with a large muslin mob cap.

"He may be older than we thought," she said thoughtfully. "He is so thin and small he only looks about eight years old, but he could be as much as twelve." She smiled again at the other girl. "We can do no more for him today. We had best make ourselves presentable for dinner. I'm sorry we did not manage to go to the shops."

Evangeline put two grimy hands to her face.

"Oh dear, I quite forgot. How could I? This is dreadful. What am I to do?"

"What did you forget? Surely it cannot be so desperate; we can go tomorrow."

Her face puckered. "Oh no, it will not be the same. You don't understand. . . ."

Miranda stared at her for some few moments and then she did understand, all too well. "You'd arranged to meet someone at the mercer's shop." Evangeline's face grew pink and she nodded her head. "Mr. Templeton?"

Evangeline looked at her appealingly. "It was all quite proper, I promise you. You would have been there and Mr. Osborne too."

Miranda felt a pang of disappointment herself and then said soothingly, "Never mind. I am sure Mr. Templeton will understand when you explain the reason. Just now I am quaking because I shall soon have to face Lord Dornford and I dread to think what he will say to me."

Evangeline hurried across to the door. "I believe he said it all this morning, Miranda."

She chuckled. "I do hope you may be right, my dear."

She was feeling extremely apprehensive by the time she went downstairs again later that day, leaving Luke still fast asleep in the truckle bed. An appetising aroma was rising from the kitchens which made Miranda aware of her hunger. The exciting events of the day had obviously given her an appetite.

Optimistically she considered it possible that her employer might stay at his club for dinner, as was so often the case, but.as she approached the library the door was standing open and when she passed a voice called out ominously, "Miss Crawley, be pleased to step in here."

She did so, closing the door behind her as he put down his quill pen and got to his feet. The desk was littered with ledgers and parchments and when she raised her eyes to his she noted he looked neither angry nor benevolent.

"Be seated, Miss Crawley."

She sank onto the edge of a chair, facing him across the desk. "Now, how is the brat?" he asked as he too sat down.

"Please don't call him that. His name is Luke and I am persuaded he has suffered all manner of hardship in his young life."

With no change in his manner he asked, "How is Luke tonight, Miss Crawley?"

"He is sleeping now and is quite comfortable."

"With two admirable females to cluck over him I would be surprised if he were not."

"Lord Dornford," she went on quickly, "I am truly grateful for what you did today and I will pay you back as promised, you need not fear."

He waved his hand in the air. "It is no great matter, I assure you."

"It is to me, you were kind enough to. . . ."

"Ten guineas is a paltry sum to me. I lose ten-fold—a hundred-fold—that amount on one card at Whites' on any evening you care to name. To you it is a great deal of money, one year's wages to be precise. I could not in all conscience take it from you."

"But if you do not, that means . . . you own him."

"I have no wish to *own* anyone, but I will certainly find suitable work for him when he has recovered his strength and shown his aptitude. It would not do for him to be idle."

She looked at him anxiously. "You will not . . . mistreat him?"

He fixed her with his disturbingly direct gaze. "No one has ever been able to accuse me of that, Miss Crawley."

She stared at her hands. "Well, be assured . . . I did not seek to burden you. . . ."

"Nevertheless you have. Your plan, well-intentioned as it was, cannot succeed. You can, through my good office, care for the bra . . . boy whilst you are here in my employ, but think on it, Miss Crawley, when you leave."

His burning gaze held hers for a moment or two and she was the first to look away. He had no way of knowing that she could well afford to do so, and the good country air of Sussex was just what he needed in those soot-choked lungs. Inevitably she did not contradict him.

"What do you know of him?" the marquis asked. "Has he spoken?"

"A little. He is extremely suspicious of our motives and . . . afraid of you."

His face remained impassive. "No doubt, in time, he will learn he has no cause—providing he does not say or do anything offensive."

"Oh, I am sure that is only caused by fear, Lord Dornford, I will make sure he does behave. He cannot recall any family. I am quite horrified."

"No doubt he was taken in off the street as a sweep's apprentice when he was an infant. Had he not, he would have surely perished anyway, so perhaps it was the lesser of the evils."

He glanced at the clock on the mantel. "It is time for dinner, I believe. This discussion is closed for now, but it may be necessary to have further talks on the subject later. You may join my sister and aunt in the drawing room now. I will be along to join you later."

Meekly Miranda got to her feet and crossed the room. When she reached the door she paused to look back. He had returned his attention to his books and papers.

"I do not know how to thank you for your generosity, Lord Dornford."

He looked up briefly. "If you deem it necessary only give me your word you will not turn my home into a benevolent society for such ragamuffins. One exceeds enough." She nodded her agreement and just as she was about to go he added, "You saved his life and I hope that brat is sensible of the fact."

"To see him safe and gaining in strength and health is all the thanks I need," she answered and she quickly left the library, closing the door behind her.

During the next few days Miranda had scant time to think about Cornelius, for she spent as much time with Luke as she could spare in an attempt to reassure him and acquaint him with his new surroundings. During that time his burns healed, the bruises faded, and due to Miranda's own concoction of honey and camomile the cough gradually disappeared too.

True to her word Lady Pendlebury procured some admirable clothes for him and when Miranda queried their origins she replied, "I have kept all my nephew's clothes, even to the extent of packing away his swaddling clothes in lavender in the hope they may be needed again—and not just for Evangeline's offspring."

"I would not set your heart too much on that, Aunt Malzena," the girl replied. "Whilst Isabella Bascome has him dazzled there is no chance of your having your wish."

"Your brother, miss, has a great deal of loyalty in him, which should not be confused with affection. Ponder on it."

"Poor Aunt Malzena," Evangeline sighed when the lady had left the room, "she never could see fault in James."

"I hardly think refusing to marry can be construed as a fault," Miranda answered, and then hesitantly asked. "Why, if he is as cynical as he seems, does he insist upon your making a marriage for love?"

"I hadn't considered it," Evangeline admitted, and then said thoughtfully, "I suppose it could be because he lost his own true love by hesitating and mayhap that is why he will not marry."

A day or two after this conversation Miranda had the unexpected opportunity to observe Isabella Bascombe at close quarters, although at first she was filled with dismay at the prospect. She was forced to admit, however, that she was curious about the woman—or rather the influence she exerted over the marquis, a man she would have thought beyond the serious influence of any woman.

It was Lady Pendlebury who deemed it time for a call on the fair Isabella, taking both Evangeline and Miranda with her in the belief that the more people present the greater would be the chance of diverting her from her wretched situation.

The three ladies arrived at the Park Lane mansion in Lord Dornford's town carriage. The house, Miranda immediately noted, was larger than Dornford House. There was a twin staircase curving up to the first floor and the walls of the great hall were painted with murals depicting the mythological stories she had read about in books belonging to her father. A negro footman in full livery led them up to the drawing room which overlooked the park itself. It was quite warm outside and yet there was a fire blazing in the hearth and the room, which was filled with gilded chairs and sofas, satinwood chests and bureaux and a great number of marquetry drum tables, was rather hot and stuffy.

Lady Bascombe reclined on a day bed near to the window so that she could see the park and the people who were constantly walking to and fro outside, but she was also protected from draughts by a silk-printed screen. At her feet squatted a negro page dressed magnificently in a tunic and a turban in the centre of which nestled a large ruby. Around his neck was the jewelled collar Evangeline had mentioned. The effect of it all was rather dazzling.

To Miranda it was strange seeing so many black-skinned servants, but she had been given to understand it was all the vogue in London.

As they entered the room Lady Bascombe stirred. "Lady Pendlebury, dear Evangeline, how kind of you to call," she said in the sweetest voice. "Come, be seated where I can see you."

Miranda hung back from the others a little, feeling rather strange but Evangeline said,

"You have not yet met Miss Crawley, Lady Bascombe."

The woman transferred her limpid gaze to Miranda. "Ah, Miss Crawley, Lord Dornford did tell me Evangeline had a friend to stay. I recall catching sight of you at the theatre and also in the park."

"I am very pleased to meet you, ma'am," she answered, bobbing a little curtsey.

"How sweet you are. You are quite lovely. Tell me, Miss Crawley, are you yet in love? I'm so isolated when I cannot venture out, quite often it's impossible to keep abreast of the news."

Taken aback by so direct a question she could only stammer inarticulately and it was Evangeline who came to her aid. "La, Lady Bascombe, Miranda has only been here a few weeks."

"I was only here two days when I first fell in love, and I can say quite truthfully since then I have never been out of love!"

Miranda averted her eyes from the woman's knowing ones. Poor Lord Bascombe, she thought, if he is truly unaware of his wife's real feelings.

The woman glanced coyly at Lady Pendlebury, who had seated herself on a nearby chair. "Has Miss Crawley entranced any *beaux* since her arrival? I am sure she ought."

Miranda felt her cheeks growing pink and

Lady Pendlebury answered gruffly, "A few, I dare say."

To Miranda's relief the conversation was interrupted by the arrival of tea. She noticed that Lady Bascombe could scarce handle the tea-kettle properly and indeed appeared to have little enough strength to raise her head from the day bed. She gave Miranda the filled cups and she was obliged to hand them round, together with the ratafia biscuits and was aware all the time that her hostess watched her carefully. It was almost as if she were on trial.

As they took tea Evangeline chattered on, conveying all the latests on-dits to the invalid and as for the most part Miranda had no idea who they were talking about she took the opportunity of studying Lady Bascombe properly for the first time.

Although she was wearing a loose robe of the palest pink she looked as beautiful as on the previous occasions Miranda had seen her, and not the slightest bit ill except for the weakness she had already noted. Her almond-shaped eyes were bright and her face well-rouged. Once again Miranda found herself marvelling at her beauty and understanding all too well the marquis's passion for this exquisite creature.

". . . and then," Lady Pendlebury was saying, "Daphne Egglesham took off her diamond ring, put it on the table and said, 'I'll wager this ring you don't do it!' whereupon Bunbury began to eat the carcass, bones and all!"

Lady Bascombe's laughter rang out merrily. "No wonder Bunbury hasn't been seen for more than a se'nnight."

"Daphne Egglesham still has her ring too," Lady Pendlebury added, then, glancing at the ormolu clock on the mantel, "We shall have to be leaving now, I'm afraid. We have stayed longer than we intended."

"You have done me the world of good, my dears, and you must call again and soon."

Lady Pendlebury got to her feet, signalling the end of the visit. "I hope you will be well re-covered enough to call on *us*."

"And attend Vauxhall," Evangeline inter-polated. "Dornford will not go if you do not."

She laughed again. "I will certainly try. I would not, for anything, spoil Dornford's fun, although he has been so good and so attentive of late it would be rather . . . foolish of me to recover *too* soon."

The others laughed and as Miranda came forward shyly Lady Bascombe looked at her again. "Miss Crawley, I fear you must have been bored by our conversation."

"On the contrary; it was interesting and amusing to hear the latest on-dits."

Her eyes sparkled. "And for once it is not about me."

Just at that moment the door was flung

open and Lord Dornford himself was announced. "I hate to interrupt your gossiping, ladies," he said mockingly as he paused in the doorway, surveying the scene before him.

"Oh, you haven't," his aunt replied, drawing on her gloves. "We were just about to go, but I am sure Isabella would be glad of your company. Come along, girls."

Miranda curtseyed. "I hope you will soon be well again, Lady Bascombe."

As Lord Dornford came further into the room the three visitors went towards the door.

"Your new addition to the household is delightful," Lady Bascombe told him.

Miranda felt herself blushing, especially when Evangeline chuckled and pinched her arm, whispering, "Lady Bascombe is quite taken by you. I can tell."

"I'm gratified you think so," the marquis answered in neutral tones, glancing quickly at Miranda and then away again.

"You are a lucky man, Dornford, a very lucky man to have a house full of such delightful females to pander your every wish."

He laughed at that. "There are times when it can be a sore trial, Isabella."

As the door closed behind them Miranda caught sight of him bending over her hand, about to kiss it. She wondered if Lady Bascombe had been sincere in her compliments or was merely being diplomatic; it was so difficult to tell. The ladies of the *ton* took delight in saying the sweetest things in front of each other whilst tearing reputations to shreds behind their backs. Miranda was glad she was not important enough to attract gossip of one kind or another.

"You that gentry-cove's missus?" Luke asked one day as Miranda sewed masks for the coming visit to Vauxhall, and he leafed disinterestedly through some magazines she had given him. He could neither read nor write, and did not wish to, but Miranda did hope to have an opportunity to teach him one day.

"If you are meaning Lord Dornford, he is not married," she answered with a laugh. "I am merely employed by him, just as you are now."

"Fearsome cove, 'e is."

"No, Luke, he is really quite kind. It is just his manner which is rather fearsome at times, but he cannot be so bad otherwise he would not have rescued you."

"Did it for you, 'e did. Saw it with me own eyes."

She was rather pleased at the thought although she did not really believe it was so; rather that the marquis was softer-hearted than he liked anyone to comprehend.

"You will just have to prove it worth his while, won't you?"

"Depends on what 'e'll 'ave me do."

"Whatever his plans for you happen to be,

you can be sure you will be clean, well-fed and kindly treated."

"Rather belong to you, missus."

Miranda was moved to discover she had his trust at last. She only hoped his evil memories would fade as fast as his bruises.

There was quite a commotion, however, when the house steward came at last to escort Luke to his new duties. He fought and kicked the poor man who was totally taken aback by such an unexpected attack.

"Luke, it is time for you to leave my side," Miranda reasoned, "but you're not going far."

"Don't want to."

"Lord Dornford wants you to work in the kitchen," she told him as he clutched at her skirts. "You are to repay his kindness by working hard and doing everything asked of you. It won't be anything too onerous I assure you."

"Want to stay with you!" he screamed, his legs and arms flailing madly as Miranda struggled to extricate herself from his grasp.

"I'll still be in the house and I'll see you often. In fact I'm going to ask permission to teach you to read and write for part of the day. Luke," she said in desperation, "If you disobey Lord Dornford he may put you out into the street again."

"Rather be in the street than down the kitchen."

"We'll see a great deal of each other, I promise you. Lord Dornford might be angry with *me* if you do not obey him."

The last threat had the desired effect and to her relief he obediently went with the steward. She sent up a little prayer that Luke would settle down well with his new work, for she knew it was not idle supposition that prompted her to say Lord Dornford's wrath would fall on her. She didn't doubt that it would for one moment.

Chapter Eight

All tickets to the masquerade at Vauxhall Gardens had been sold weeks before the event, and every box in the Rotunda was occupied almost without exception by illustrious personages dressed magnificently beneath dominoes and masks, many of them jewelled and extravagantly fashioned.

Occupying a box in a prime position from which everyone who entered the Rotunda could be viewed, Miranda was enjoying herself far more than on the first occasion she had visited the pleasure gardens with Evangeline and her aunt. On this occasion she was at least acquainted with many of the people present and it was great fun trying to recognise them behind their masks, many of which covered the entire face.

A band played on a dais for those who wished to dance or merely listen. Earlier the assembled company had enjoyed a display by jugglers, acrobats and tumblers, all of whom had amazing dexterity, and now, having been joined by Cornelius and Myles as well as several other young people of their acquaintance, they were partaking of some supper.

Miranda was moved as Cornelius thoughtfully procured a plateful of cold ham and chicken for her. Since the night of Lord Dornford's rout she had scarce seen him but the blame was hers; she had been so occupied with Luke of late. Now he seemed to be settled in the kitchen, devouring, Cook had informed her, every left-over scrap. Happily, he need not take all her attention in the future and she could concentrate at last on her own love life when she was not attending Evangeline.

There were times when Miranda considered all the advantages of the position she held were on her side, but when a slight pricking of conscience had prompted her to say so to Evangeline one day, the girl discounted the idea immediately.

"I think of you as a sister," she had declared, "and a particularly indulgent one at that," which had the effect of making Miranda experience both gladness and remorse.

"Mr. Templeton," Evangeline was saying, smiling sweetly at Miranda's brother who, as always of late, was not far from the girl's side, "do you think I might have just a little more of the venison pasty?"

Miranda was amazed to see how quickly

Myles went to fulfill the command; he had always scorned gentlemen who danced attendance upon ladies of the *ton*, but before she could muse on it further her attention was diverted by Cornelius who said in a low whisper,

"I have scarce had a moment to speak to you since the rout, Miranda. I have been quite concerned about how you fared with Lord Dornford. Did he suspect anything was amiss?"

"Oh no, not at all," she hastened to reply, giving him an assured smile. "I was able to make an adequate excuse for being out there."

"I was disappointed when you and Lady Evangeline did not arrive at the mercer's on Tuesday. We waited for a full hour before conceding you would not come."

"Something unavoidable happened. We both regretted the missed opportunity."

Reproachfully he said, "It seems I have had so few opportunities of seeing you of late."

"That is because I have been occupied with a small boy called Luke." She went on to explain the circumstances and his eyes grew round.

"Really, Miranda, a sweep's brat, it isn't the thing!" he complained when she had finished.

"If only you could have seen him, Cornelius, your heart would have been moved too but now he looks so bonny. It does my heart good to see him. He will work hard and repay our confidence in him."

"Our?"

"Without Lord Dornford's help it could not have been achieved."

Mr. Osborne made a sound of annoyance and Miranda noticed that Evangeline was looking at them with interest. "I have been telling Mr. Osborne all about Luke," she explained to her.

Evangeline dimpled. "That is quite a story, Mr. Osborne," she said before returning her attention to Myles.

"We really cannot talk properly in here," Cornelius complained a moment later.

"We must have a care, Cornelius. I should hate to repeat what happened at the rout."

He waved his hand in a gesture of irritation. "That is unlikely. Lord Dornford isn't here tonight and even if he were Vauxhall is so crowded we would neither be missed nor be seen. We have the added advantage of being masked."

"I would know you anywhere."

He smiled. "And I you, but Dornford would not know his sister's companion. Later we must meet in one of the dark walks. Unlike Dornford House, Vauxhall is made for such assignations."

Miranda gave him a sharp look although because she was masked she doubted if he would know of it. "Not between ladies and gentlemen of breeding, Cornelius."

"Especially so."

She toyed with her food. "No. I cannot.

After the other evening I have decided we
must only meet in the normal way. I have de-
ceived Evangeline and Lord Dornford enough.
In all conscience I cannot do it any longer."

"Do you intend to confess all to them?"

Startled Miranda retorted, "Oh no. I just
wish to do my duty and behave in as straight-
forward manner as I can."

He looked furious but she affected not to notice it and continued to eat her supper although she now had little taste for it. On his
way to replenish Evangeline's plate with more
pasty Myles paused by them and said in a low
voice, "Beware, Miranda, Lady Berriman is
approaching the box."

She turned in alarm to see four masked people approaching. "How can you tell it is Lady
Berriman?" she asked in amazement.

He chuckled. "Her mask is in the form of a
serpent's head. It can be none other."

The lady inclined her head imperiously to all
those in the box, exchanged a few trite remarks
with Lady Pendlebury who had up until then
been lost in a game of vingt-et-un with her
friend, the duchess, and two other cronies, and
then she turned her attention to Miranda
whose spirits sank.

"So, you are still residing in London, Miss
Crawley."

Miranda swallowed noisily and answered,
"Yes, ma'am."

"I have been meaning to ask; are you by any

chance related to Sir Sebastian Crawley of Cheltenham Spa? There is a look about you. . . ."

"No, ma'am," she answered in a choked voice and to her profound relief Myles said, "Lady Berriman, will you do me the honour of standing up with me for this quadrille?"

Immediately diverted she said in a voice filled with pleasure, "Certainly, Myles," and as Miranda sighed with relief and sank back into her chair she could imagine the flush of delight on the woman's face beneath the mask.

Cornelius also got to his feet. "Miss Berriman, may I also be honoured?"

Millicent Berriman simpered and giggled as Cornelius turned back to Miranda and whispered, "Meet me at the grotto after the quadrille is finished."

"I will not," she hissed.

He leaned closer. "If you do not I shall tell everyone who you are and declare my love for you. So be warned. This ruse has lasted long enough."

Frustrated and angry Miranda watched him go. Oh why, oh why did I come here? she asked herself, but at the same time knew she was glad she had.

As the dance ended she watched Cornelius escort Millicent Berriman back to her mother's box and then making her excuses made her exit. Evangeline was holding court with her admirers, Lady Pendlebury intent upon her card game and Miranda was certain none of them noticed she had gone.

Most of the pleasure gardens was lit by thousands of lanterns suspended in the trees and hanging from the triumphal arches, but there were dark walks too where lovers could meet, and thieves and pickpockets roamed. Many a drunken buck returned home without his purse from an evening at Vauxhall.

As she hurried along the paths there were drunks aplenty lying senseless in the bushes or staggering along, and characters lurking in the long shadows who looked as though they could be felons. She did not like walking unescorted, for many of the bucks she passed eyed her with undue interest, mistaking her motives in being there. It was with some relief that she approached the grotto and saw Cornelius waiting in the shadows.

"I fear that was close call with Lady Berriman," he said with a laugh.

Miranda was, however, in no mood to be humoured. "How dare you threaten me," she said without preamble.

His smile of welcome faded. "Miranda, I did not mean. . . ."

"I meant what *I* said. I refuse to meet you in these circumstances ever again, and if you dare to threaten me with exposure I shall inform Myles of it and let him deal with you."

He took her hand in his and raised it to his

lips. "I would not wish to hurt you; you must know that. Only, when shall we meet? Not surely with everyone else as witness. It is not to be borne."

"But it's the only proper way. If Myles was aware of our secret meeting he would be outraged, and rightly so."

Suddenly a hard look came over his face and a steely look into his eyes. "If you'd been concerned with what was proper, you would not have come to London."

Her head drooped. "I know," she answered in a strangled voice. "I was not aware of the pressures I would have to endure."

"You did not explain clearly how you came to be acquainted with Lord Dornford. It seems to me to be a most curious business."

She cleared her throat. "There is no time for that now, Cornelius. It must almost be time for the fireworks and unmasking, and we shall have to return to the box."

"I care nothing for that," he said catching her other hand. "The only person I want to be with is you, and now we are here let us make the most of it."

For the first time Miranda felt embarrassed. "We *must* go. We do not want to cause the others to speculate."

"Don't you see, Miranda?" he said in urgent tones. "It doesn't matter any more. If anyone does speculate, you have been here long enough now for me to be able to attend you with no suspicion. It will appear quite normal."

"A paid companion, Cornelius?"

"Let people say I am a fool," he answered laughingly. "You are beautiful enough for everyone to understand my madness. If only I had realised my true feelings before I left Sussex."

Withdrawing her hands from his she said, "I . . . would rather you did not do anything rash now. I will as soon as I am properly able return home and perhaps you and Myles will rusticate again this summer. Then we can begin anew, Cornelius, in the correct way. There is nothing romantic about secret meetings although in truth I thought that there might be."

His face took on a woebegon expression. "The summer! That is a long time hence and Myles will not leave Evangeline's side now."

She laughed. "Oh, that is of no account. It is only because. . . ."

"Yes, Miranda?"

"Oh nothing," she said quickly, looking away.

She began to turn away but he caught her by the shoulders. "Have you forgotten you came here to be with me, Miranda, not as a servant to Evangeline Devilliars and her brother?"

Fireworks began to explode in the sky above them, green, blue and red, accompanied by shrieks of delight from the visitors.

Miranda gasped and said in desperation. "We must return to the box lest the others wonder why we are not there."

"I have told you, I would as lief declare myself now."

"Oh, Cornelius," she begged, "if you truly care for me please do not. I am so confused. This is neither the time nor the place to decide our future." She pushed him away from her. "Go that way and I will return the way I came. We will talk at a more appropriate time. *Hurry*."

"Miranda. . . .!"

She paid no heed to him. Lifting her skirts she fled back along the path, passing people who were gasping in admiration at the firework display which she had not yet noticed properly.

What is wrong with me? she asked herself as tears pricked at her eyes. I have achieved my heart's desire. Why do I not want Cornelius's love now?

When she came to a lighter part of the pathway she slowed her pace and paused to compose herself. When I am back home it will be different, she promised.

A group of fashionable young men were ahead of her and she started to walk more decorously. It was only when she got closer to the group that she hesitated once more, recognising the broad back of one of them. That arrogant stance, she thought in alarm, can belong to only one person.

She would have turned and gone back the way she had come even though it meant moving further away from the Rotunda which she longed to reach, but one of the group took an interest in her and moments later every one of them was staring in her direction and she had no choice but to go on. Pulling the domino closer around her and the hood around her face she walked slowly forward, her heart beating fast with apprehension. Alone and unaccompanied it was no wonder they mistook her for one of the many harlots who frequented the place.

With her face averted she drew level with them and quickened her pace. One of them, who she now recognised as a viscount of the marquis's acquaintance, shouted "Don't be so bashful, my beauty. Time for unmasking." He seemed considerably the worse for drink.

Miranda did not hesitate but the buck who had spoken caught hold of her arm. "Tarry a while," he coaxed. "You shall not regret it."

"Please let me go," she pleaded, aware that the marquis was leaning against a trellis watching with some amusement.

"Hurrying to your lover, eh?" queried the viscount thickly. "You'll find me a better benefactor."

"I wish to return to my friends, sir," she answered, willing herself to remain calm.

"Shame!" mocked one of the others.

Before she had a chance to realise what was happening her arm was freed from the viscount's and caught in the marquis's vice-like grip instead. Miranda whirled round in alarm to face him. He was smiling cruelly and she was as much afraid of him as she was that night at the "Bell". By revealing her identity she would save herself further humiliation at his hand, but only at the cost of inviting his disgust and this she could not bring herself to do.

"Please unhand me, sir," she begged, her voice no more than a whisper.

"You don't escape so fast," he answered laughing harshly and tightening his grip on her wrist. "I have a fancy," he mused, "there is a real beauty in disguise here. It is long past the time for unmasking so let me be honoured to look upon the face so unjustly hidden."

The others were laughing and urging him on but as he reached for the ribbons of her mask she jerked her head away.

With her breast heaving with indignation she said, "You mistake me, sir. Please let me join my friends in their box."

"Oh, you shall certainly go to your unworthy friends but first let me look upon a face I believe to be more than fair. Those eyes cannot lie and neither can your lips."

She struggled and managed to prevent him removing the mask, something she attributed to his state of mild intoxication. "You must be drunk."

"Most delightfully so, but I refuse to believe this meeting is a figment of my drunken imagination. It cannot be."

The others had lost interest and were setting off in pursuit of some painted harlots who had flounced by, flashing inviting looks at them. As they departed Miranda felt even more desperate and afraid.

"Your lips are those of an innocent, as yet unawakened. If I cannot look upon your face allow me one kiss."

She shrank away but he gripped her so tightly she could scarcely move.

"I must," he said hungrily, "have one kiss before you go. This cannot be too much to ask for my sacrifice."

Miranda pushed her hands against his chest but his strength was too much for her. She struggled but he did kiss her and with no tenderness or consideration. It went on and suddenly she was no longer struggling in his arms. The fireworks had ceased, but she was not aware of that; it seemed as if they still exploded but this time in her head.

At last he released her and with brutal abruptness. "Now you may go," he said hoarsely. "Whosoever takes advantage of the innocence of your lips in the future, I am certain you will never forget this occasion."

Turning on his heel he hurried away from

her. Miranda, still bewildered and totally bemused, watched him disappear into the dark-
ness and then, lifting her skirts, she ran
headlong towards the Rotunda.

Chapter Nine

Everyone slept late the following morning, everyone except for Miranda, that is. She felt she had not slept at all and was not likely to do so again.

It was fortunate that the party decided to depart from Vauxhall shortly after her return to the box, for she was certain the others would notice her agitation and preoccupation.

Guilt racked her as she paced the floor of her bedroom, reliving the events of the previous evening. Why hadn't Cornelius's kiss affected her in such a devastating way? She told herself kisses should not affect well-reared young ladies in the way Lord Dornford's kiss had disturbed her, and she determined to put it from her mind once and for all.

When she finally composed herself sufficiently to go down to breakfast she rejoiced in the fact that he had no idea who he had kissed, otherwise she would not have been able to face him again. Even so she fervently hoped he would not be present at breakfast or around the house that day. It would be all she could do to concentrate on Evangeline's chatter, knowing she would wish to discuss the events of the previous evening and examine every moment of it in detail.

The library door was half open as she approached and she would have gone past quickly only a high-pitched cry arrested her. Her eyes grew wide in alarm as the cry came again. It was almost certainly Luke's voice that she had heard.

Hesitantly she pushed the door open and went a little way inside, ready to scold the boy for trespassing on Lord Dornford's private domain, but she gasped in surprise at the sight of him cowering in the corner. The marquis, for once downstairs in his shirtsleeves, was towering over him, brandishing a stick menacingly.

"Lord Dornford!" she cried. "What are you doing to him?"

At this he transferred his attention to Miranda and she recoiled at the blind fury on his face. "Not as much as I am going to do," he answered.

Seeing Miranda, the boy rushed towards her, clinging on to her skirts. "Gave me a lickin', 'e did," he sobbed.

She put one hand on his head but looked at the marquis reproachfully. "Lord Dornford, you promised."

"Shouldn't you first ask what prompted me

to give him a beating, or is anything he is like to do permissible with you?" Before she had a chance to reply he walked across to the desk. "Look at this," he commanded and Miranda moved forward to do so.

A portion of the desk was littered with several objects. She recognised the marquis's diamond pin near a few of his collection of silver, gold and porcelain snuff boxes. She also recognised a bracelet belonging to Evangeline and several rings which she had last seen adorning Lady Pendlebury's fingers.

"Do you recognise them?" the marquis asked in a carefully controlled voice.

"Most certainly I do."

"I missed the diamond pin this morning and sent my valet to this wretch's attic and sure enough these objects were immediately found to be beneath his mattress."

"Oh Luke," she sighed. "Why *did* you do it, you naughty boy?"

Luke wiped his tear-streaked face on her skirt and then looked up at her. "Wanted them for you. You've got nothin'. They'm 'ave a lot."

Miranda gazed down at him. "Did I not tell you it is wrong to steal? Did you imagine I would accept them from you?"

"Platitudes," the marquis said irritably. "Am I to lock up every valuable in my own house?"

She looked at him appealingly. "I am sure he will not take anything again." She took hold of him by the arms and made him stand up straight. "Promise me you will never do anything like this again."

"He will not have the opportunity," Lord Dornford promised darkly and her heart sank.

"Too late now, ain't it?" the boy cried. " 'is nibs'll 'ave me up before the beak and I'll be nubbed next 'anging day."

Miranda cried out in alarm and then looked appealingly at the marquis. Her embarrassment over the previous night was completely forgotten.

"Please tell him you will not do anything of the kind."

"He deserves no better." After a moment or two he averted his eyes from hers. "Very well," he said with a sigh. "It is clear he cannot be held responsible for this, for he does not know what is right and what is wrong. Come over here, boy."

Luke remained clinging to Miranda's skirts but she said, "Do as you are bid. You have nothing to fear from Lord Dornford."

The boy obviously did not believe her but he slowly went to stand before his master who continued to look down upon him severely.

"Mark carefully what I say. You will *not* be sent to Newgate—on this occasion, but let there be no repeat of this. . . ." he waved his hand over the desk. "Miss Crawley does not need you to steal for her. Is that understood?" The boy slowly nodded. "You may return to your duties now." Gratefully the boy rushed to the door and when he reached it the marquis added, "Miss Crawley has an inordinate amount of faith in you. Do not disappoint her again or most certainly you will answer for it severely."

Miranda let out a long sigh of relief and when Luke had gone she said softly, "Thank you, Lord Dornford."

"One does not thank a lunatic, Miss Crawley, for that is what I must be to allow such occurrences to happen in my house." Her lips curved into a smile but when he looked up at her it quickly disappeared again. "We must discuss his future. Please sit down."

As she did so she said demurely, "It is not for me to say what his future is to be."

He smiled wryly. "If you truly believe that, you must be very naive. Now," he said briskly, seating himself behind the desk and stretching his legs out beneath it, "it is not possible for him to remain here."

At Miranda's muted, "Oh," he went on quickly, "I shall arrange for him to be taken to my country estate in Oxfordshire where he can learn to work usefully, perhaps with animals; children usually enjoy being with animals and we must remember he is only a child." He glanced at her quickly and then away again. "My mind is quite made up, Miss Crawley, so do not subject me to floods of tears. They will have no effect, so do not think to send Evangeline to plead his case either."

"I would not dream of doing so, Lord Dornford. The good country air may be just what he needs. Inhaling soot for so many years has weakened his chest somewhat and I am afraid he may never be robust."

The marquis seemed somewhat taken aback and said gruffly, "Well, now that is decided you may go. There is nothing more to discuss. I leave it to you to impress upon the boy this course is for his own good."

Miranda was halfway across the room when she hesitated. He was sitting back in his chair, gazing at her sombrely, his arms folded in front of him. "The only pity is," she said as lightly as she could, "I had hoped to be able to teach him to read and write before I leave."

He smiled slightly. "You may yet have the opportunity. The summer fast approaches. Once the Season is over, I might just decide to engage you as governess to the brat."

She parted her lips to say something but no words issued forth.

"Congenial posts are not so easy to secure, Miss Crawley, and I do believe you have been happy here."

"Oh yes," she answered in heartfelt tones.

"Then you would welcome the opportunity of remaining in my employ?"

"I . . . would . . . prefer to discuss the matter at a later date, Lord Dornford. May I have your permission to go now?"

"You have it," he said curtly and she hurried from the room, gulping back her tears until she reached the hall and she could contain them no longer. She leaned back against the wall and sobbed heartbrokenly. She lost track of time, knowing she could bear the pretence no longer. However considerable were the marquis's faults, she could not continue to deceive him, but neither could she return to the library and confess. Her life at that moment was intolerable.

She straightened up as a footman came down the corridor and she began to fumble with her handkerchief. Just as that moment the breakfast room door opened and she averted her face. Evangeline gasped when she caught sight of her companion.

"Miranda, oh Miranda, here you are! Have you heard what Luke has done? What a lark! Dornford is furious, but you must allow it is vastly amusing." She looked more closely at Miranda then. "You have been weeping! Oh, has my brother given you a set down over this?"

Miranda shook her head ferociously and blew her nose. "No, he has been extraordinarily generous over Luke's misdemeanour, far more than the child deserves, and that is what has moved me so, Evangeline."

The girl looked surprised. "I declare it is quite unlike him."

Lady Pendlebury came hurrying down the stairs at that moment. "La! You two girls are abroad early today. Well, you look bright enough which is a blessing, for we shall be able to attend Lady Dennison's luncheon party after all." She peered at them both. "By the by, has either of you girls seen my garnet ring? I must be growing absentminded, for I cannot find it anywhere."

"In the library, Aunt Malzena," Evangeline said demurely and at the look of astonishment on the woman's face both girls burst into laughter.

As the days passed Miranda found that although the house was somewhat quieter she did not miss Luke as much as she had feared, for her time was filled with unending activity. Her latest attack of guilt and remorse did not abate overmuch and the sight of Evangeline's constant ebullience did nothing to help it do so, for she feared it was none other than Myles who had caused it.

She longed for a coze with her brother, but as was so often the case of late he was leading a hectic social life of his own which invariably involved the lovely Evangeline. As for Cornelius, Miranda spent much of her time keeping him at arm's length, for she was now certain the fondness she felt for him was not an enduring love. At home he had appeared the epitome of sophistication but here in London he merged into a veritable tapestry of like young men. He, she was sure, suspected her change of heart, but she dare not make it plain to him for fear that he might be rash enough to denounce her as the fraud she was.

Such thoughts were constantly in her mind now and although she knew Evangeline would be puzzled and hurt, it was the marquis's reaction she feared most of all. He was not a man to tolerate the trickery she had perpetrated, even though she was consoled by the knowledge that it was he who had forced her into this situation, a role she had fulfilled to the best of her ability.

But Evangeline's current attachment to Myles (something Miranda blamed herself for wholeheartedly) was in the forefront of her mind too, and it was on the morning after a particularly late homecoming that Miranda's worst fears were finally confirmed.

Up and dressed at the usual time, she went along to Evangeline's bedchamber to find the girl, as expected, still in her bed, but sitting up and sipping at her chocolate. Jenny, her maid, was busily setting out her mistress's clothes in preparation for the day ahead.

"How can you be up so early," Evangeline complained as Miranda entered the room.

"Rising early is a lifetime's habit which I cannot break, and it *is* almost eleven o'clock."

Evangeline, angelically clad in a white nightgown lavishly adorned with Brussell's lace, a cap covering her dark curls, patted the silk counterpane.

"Come talk with me, Miranda. Wasn't it the most wonderful evening? My feet scarce touched the ground."

"It was very enjoyable," she agreed. "You looked magnificent. Your gown was the envy of all those present."

The girl dimpled. "I received a score of compliments to be sure, but you looked wonderful too. You perform miracles with that needle of yours. I declare, if you were not employed as a companion you would succeed as a mantua-maker to the *ton*."

Miranda laughed. "It's comforting to know I need never starve for the want of employment."

"I assure you that will never occur whilst I am able to aid you."

She had to look away, saying in a choked voice, "Such sentiments mean more than you know, but you need have no worry on my account, my dear, for I shall always contrive."

"I shall see that you do!" A moment later she said pensively, "Do you think that Dornford has mellowed slightly of late?"

Such a question caused Miranda to look up

sharply. "Mellow is not a word I would use to describe Lord Dornford, Evangeline."

"Lately he has accompanied us to engagements which would have certainly bored him not long ago."

"No doubt they still do. It may just be he has become sensible of his duty towards you."

"He always was," she answered artlessly. "No one could wish for a dearer brother." Miranda did not, of course, contradict her and a moment later she went on thoughtfully, "It may come to pass that he will marry after all. I noted his attention to Fanny Haygarth last night, and it was not for the first time. Aunt Malzena would like it if he fixed his interest in that direction. She thinks the line should continue direct and Fanny's mother is one of Aunt Malzena's cronies."

Miranda too had noticed the marquis's attention to the pretty but rather vapid girl. "But what . . . about Lady Bascombe?"

Evangeline laughed merrily. "Goose, as if that need make any difference." As Miranda's face registered shock Evangeline went on in a matter-of-fact way, "Of course it is possible that Dornford has grown tired of Isabella; she ails so much these days. My brother is loyal as Aunt Malzena pointed out but he is also easily out of patience and not the type to dance attendance on the sick room. I recall once he kept some creature in a house in Mount Street until she began to demand more of his time than he was willing to give." She looked at Miranda's stony face and said mischievously, "Enough about Dornford, for I know you and my brother do not exactly get on famously together."

"Please don't think that, Evangeline," Miranda protested. "It isn't true."

"That is a great relief. I do so want you to like each other. I noticed last night that Mr. Osborne was scarce from your side the entire evening, and it was not the first time I had noted it."

In some alarm Miranda got to her feet. "No! You are quite mistaken. Mr. Osborne . . . well surely being close to me is the next best thing to being with you."

"I do not believe that for one moment. He harboured some affection for me at one time, but now he is in earnest over you. I am convinced of it. Would it not be famous if he offered for you?"

She pressed her hands to her lips. "No, Evangeline, it would not, for I would be bound to refuse him and that would be distressing."

"Miranda," she said in dismay. "You cannot know what you mean! Mr. Osborne has expectations. His grandfather is the Earl of Heldon."

Miranda turned to look out of the window. In her agitation, unconsciously she was tugging at her sash. "It makes no odds to me if he were heir to a dukedom."

At this Evangeline could no longer remain motionless in bed. She swung her legs over the side of the bed.

"Miranda, I must try to make you see sense in this matter. In your situation the chance of another eligible young man coming along is remote, if not impossible. Forgive me if I say you cannot afford to pick and choose where you will."

"I do not wish to seem ungrateful—to anyone—but I am adamant I shall marry only for love and I do not love Mr. Osborne."

There was a momentary silence before the girl sighed deeply. "You have no notion how much I admire you for that, Miranda. I admit in your place I should not have the courage to refuse him, especially as he is so pleasing."

Smiling and composed once more Miranda turned on her heel. "He has not asked and may never do so."

Evangeline smiled too. "Such matters are of great concern to me at the moment, so you must forgive my zeal. Miranda, can you keep a secret?"

"I've always been held to do so."

"I believe Mr. Templeton is about to offer for me."

The smile froze on her lips and the room began to swim before her eyes. Evangeline's face took on a look of concern and she hurried to her.

"My dear, you have turned so pale. What ails you?"

"Nothing, nothing," she murmured as Evangeline helped her to a chair. Miranda thankfully sat down and said in a strangled voice, "You do not intend to accept."

"Oh, I do. Do you feel better? These late nights take more toll of you than you will admit. Shall I fetch a vinaigrette?" Miranda shook her head and Evangeline went on in a gentle voice, "I know what ails you, Miranda."

"You do?"

"You need not fear for your position. Oh, I know Dornford only engaged you for the Season, but I could not let you go now. If you do not wish to marry then I want you to stay with me for ever. I will never abandon *you*."

Once more uncharacteristically near to tears Miranda said, "Let us not discuss this now. Tell me how you can be certain that Mr. Templeton will offer for you."

She had never felt so wretched than at that moment when she looked into Evangeline's glowing face. "I know it, Miranda. When one is in love, as I am, it is an instinct. I pray that one day you will know what it is like to experience this rapture."

"Do you . . . know anything about him . . . his family?"

"Enough. We have spoken about such matters from time to time. He is Sir William Templeton's heir. They have a considerable parcel of land in the south. His father," she went on in a confiding voice, "is something of an eccentric. He had been trying to write a definitive history of the world for the past eight years. Myles," she blushed, "Mr. Templeton says he will never live to complete it, but it is an all-consuming passion with him and he will not be deflected from the purpose. It is his poor sister I pity. She is only twenty but is forced to care for her father and the house with no social life of her own."

Miranda stared down at her hands. She would have been tempted to strangle her brother had he been in the room at that moment. She had not given him leave to go so far. These confidences went beyond what was bearable.

"Once we are married I shall make sure she enjoys our social life too and does not become an old maid, which will be her fate if someone does not come to her aid. It will be my first task when we return from our honeymoon trip."

"You may not like her."

Evangeline laughed delightedly. "She is Mr. Templeton's twin sister, so I will love her even if she is as plain as a pipe-stem, and I cannot conceive how that can be." The girl looked suddenly sober. "Miranda, you do like Mr. Templeton don't you? That is very important to me, for I value your opinion greatly. Recall that he was kind to you when you first arrived."

Miranda affected a warm smile. "I hold him in very high regard, none more so, but you are very young and there are so many others. . . ."

"For me there is only one," she said dreamily. "No one else comes close to him in stature."

"But, Evangeline, you may have mistaken him," Miranda said in desperation.

"I could not mistake such ardour."

Miranda could do or say no more on the subject so she merely leaned over and kissed her cheek. "My dear, I do wish you every happiness in the world."

Satisfied, Evangeline hurried across the room. "I must dress immediately. There is so much to do and we are to go shopping with Aunt Malzena today." As she threw off her nightgown she called to Miranda, "Will you do my hair today? The last time you dressed it for me Mr. Templeton admired it greatly."

Drawing a deep sigh Miranda got to her feet. "Of course I will dress your hair for you. Where is your powdering robe. . . .?"

Chapter Ten

At just about the time the three ladies were setting out on their shopping expedition Lord Dornford was sauntering slowly along Bond Street, having just settled an outstanding bill with his wine shipper and placed a further order for brandy and claret. He was musing on how soon after his last order it had become necessary to replenish his stocks of wine when a landau drew level with him and on seeing Lady Berriman accompanied by two of her daughters inside it he paused to raise his hat.

"Good morning, ladies," he said, bestowing upon them an easy smile which caused both Millicent and Constance to giggle and pinch each other.

Flashing her daughters a look of displeasure the countess returned his smile. "Good morning, Lord Dornford. It is well that I have seen you, for I was wondering how dear Lady Bascombe fared at present."

"Not very well, I'm afraid. Not well at all.

Lord Bascombe has engaged a physician from Paris and I am on my way to their house now to learn his diagnosis."

"You must be very anxious to arrive there with as little delay as possible so perhaps you will allow me to take you there. It is on our way."

"That is exceedingly kind of you." As the lackey jumped down to open the door Lady Berriman urged her girls to move up to make more room for the marquis.

"I was, in fact, hoping to find a moment of your time, Lady Berriman," he said as the carriage started forward.

"I am honoured indeed."

"It cannot have escaped your notice that my sister has formed an attachment to a young man of your acquaintance. . . ."

"Mr. Templeton," she answered smugly. "He is my god-son."

"Precisely. You realise then why I wish to have words with you in private?"

The woman flustered slightly and he went on as the two girls gazed at him wide-eyed and open-mouthed. "My sister's happiness is of the greatest import to me and I wish to ascertain that there is no cause for me to . . . discourage him."

"Oh no, indeed, Lord Dornford. Myles Templeton is the dearest, sweetest boy one could wish to meet. He has always behaved towards me and the girls with the utmost respect. You need have no qualms about his suitability."

The marquis stroked his chin thoughtfully. "There is little in the way of family, I understand. . . ."

"His poor dear mama was my dearest friend, but she passed on some ten years ago. Their father, I regret to say," she added, bristling slightly, "is a mite. . . ."

"Eccentric," he supplied.

She smiled. "Just so, Lord Dornford. He believes he must write a history of the world and has devoted himself to doing so for several years—much to the detriment of his children, may I add."

"Children?"

"Myles has a sister. Her name is in fact Lenore; she was named for me. *She*, of course resides with Sir William."

"She has not had her come-out?"

Lady Berriman met his eyes which were questioning and she started a little. "Why no, Lord Dornford. Naturally, as she has no mother and no other female relatives a Season is not easy to arrange." He continued to look at her and she felt bound to continue, "I would have launched her myself and may yet do so, only . . . well, her father is so difficult to deal with and . . . I do have my own girls to settle. It is my beholden duty to do right by them first. And to be frank, Lord Dornford, Lenore has always been rather hoydenish. She may be

Myles's twin, but in nature and character they are quite unalike. As children Lenore led Myles by the nose into no end of scrapes. I have always feared she would influence my own dear girls to transgress."

He stared at them so hard they felt bound to cling to each other, and then their mother said, "You may be sure I *will* do my duty to her once the girls are settled."

"Perhaps Miss Templeton cannot wait that long," the marquis said dryly.

Lady Berriman looked outraged. "I beg your pardon, Lord Dornford."

The marquis turned the full force of his charming smile on her. "I merely meant that the girl must be twenty years old now."

"Oh indeed," she mused, mollified once more. "How time does fly."

"As a matter of interest, how long is it since you last saw her?"

"Let me see; why I believe it is all of ten years, Lord Dornford."

"That is a considerable time."

"I have had my own family to care for in that time. Dorinda is not yet out of the schoolroom."

"It is entirely possible you will not recognise her."

Lady Berriman laughed harshly. "Lord Dornford, with that red hair and those bold insolent eyes, it is well-nigh impossible! Truth to tell, I am surprised that one with Lenore's spirit has endured rusticating so long. She was never one to allow Myles far from her sphere of influence for long." She smiled warmly. "Of course, if Lady Evangeline does marry my godson—and I don't believe I am presuming too much—I am convinced she will take delight in launching the girl."

The carriage had reached the house on Park Lane and came to a halt outside it. Lord Dornford began to get out, saying, "From what you have told me, Lady Berriman, I believe it just possible that Miss Templeton has been spirited enough to make her own arrangements in that particular matter. I thank you for your confidence. It has been most informative talking with you. Good day to you, ladies."

The girls giggled again before chorusing in answer to their mother's ferocious look, "Good day, Lord Dornford."

Lady Berriman put her head out of the window, which was rather difficult as she wore a broad-brimmed hat liberally adorned with feathers on top of her elaborate hair-style. "It has been a pleasure to talk with *you*, Lord Dornford. You must join us for breakfast one day next week. I shall send an invitation. After all," she added coyly, "we may soon be related, so to speak."

The marquis drew a deep sigh which escaped the lady's notice for he smiled back at her most charmingly.

"And do convey my good wishes to poor Lady Bascombe."

"I will certainly do so," he answered as the carriage started up again.

Immediately Lady Berriman's smile faded as she rounded on her daughters, lashing out at the poor creatures with her cane. "Imbeciles!" She took a pinch of snuff which in her agitation spilled onto the skirt of her gown. "Lord Dornford condescended to honour us with his presence and all you can do is giggle! What am I to do with you? Constance, you are almost nineteen and unmarried still. Evangeline Devilliars is not yet eighteen and this is her first season—she will be wed before you!" She brushed at the snuff with an agitated hand. "Lord Dornford is one of the most eligible bachelors in the kingdom and it is like that Fanny Haygarth will bring him up to scratch. What a lost opportunity. Bah!"

She rapped on the coachman's back with her cane. "Take us home!"

"But we were to buy new bonnets, Mama," Constance complained.

"The finest frills and furbelows will not improve you. I may as well save the blunt. If you insist on putting off any eligible man with your simpering you will need it!"

"Why do you suddenly wish to return home now, Miranda?" Myles asked, pushing his hands distractedly through his hair.

He was pacing the floor of the parlour in his lodging house, still clad in his frogged dressing gown. Miranda had known the only opportunity to speak with him would be early in the morning whilst the others were still in bed, and she had taken a rare chance to slip out unseen.

"Because I must," she answered in a subdued voice.

"You came because of Cornelius. What of him now?"

Miranda stared down at her clasped hands. "I don't love him, Myles. You may be sure of that. I am afraid he will reveal my identity before long."

"He will not. *You* may be sure of that, so you can stay."

"No, dearest," she answered wearily. "It was not solely a fear of Cornelius's indiscretion which prompted me. I have been considering my position for a while."

A muscle at the side of his mouth contracted and his hands clenched into fists at his side. "Dornford has not been . . . plaguing you, has he? He will have me to contend with if he has."

She gave a broken little laugh. "No, he does not even see me most of the time, even when I am in the room."

"Then what can have occurred to put you in such a pucker?"

"I did not mind the pretence whilst no one stood in risk of being harmed by it, but it has gone too far I fear. I cannot bear the consequences any longer."

He sat down on the edge of a chair and peered at her. "Who is in danger of being harmed?"

She looked up at him at last. "Evangeline."

He stiffened. "Evangeline! What do you mean by that?"

"Myles, I did wrong to ask you to pay her court just to satisfy my own selfish whims. In mitigation, with so many men begging for her favours, I had no idea she would take it so seriously, but you must cease now, Myles! She believes you about to offer for her."

"She is correct. I shall speak to her brother as soon as the opportunity arises. Today if possible."

"Myles!"

"I wished to tell you sooner, only there has been scant opportunity."

"You do not love her!"

He looked beyond her and his eyes became misty. "No, I do not love her; I adore her and worship the very earth she walks upon. Her voice is like heavenly music when she speaks, and her laughter is like the tinkling of silver bells."

Miranda stared at him in astonishment. "I cannot credit this. You reviled her so much. . . ."

"I did not know her then. I was totally ignorant of her true worth. Oh, Miranda, she is so sweet and loving, and she looks like an angel. Does she truly love me? I dared not hope. . . ."

"She declares she is madly in love with you."

Unable to contain his joy any further he jumped to his feet. "This is wonderful news! Miranda, I am the happiest man in the whole world." He turned to her excitedly. "Do you not realise it is to you whom I owe this? If it were not for you I might never have had the opportunity to know her, let alone love her. Do say you love her too."

Her eyes were moist with tears. "Dearest, you know I do. And I do wish you happy, if indeed Dornford will accept your offer."

"Evangeline has given me every reason to believe that he will. She has hinted as much and by now he should be well aware of her wishes. Do you know, Miranda?" he added thoughtfully, "Dornford isn't really a bad sort of a fellow after all."

"I am in agreement with you upon that point," she answered in a carefully controlled voice.

"And it will be wonderful to have you here with me when the announcement is made, even though we cannot acknowledge the connection."

Feeling distressed again she answered, "Oh, I cannot remain until then, Myles."

"You must. I wish it, dearest, and there is no pressing need for you to leave now. You are my only relative save Papa, who will not attend.

Evangeline too will be devastated if you leave at this particularly happy time."

"She will be even more devastated if she discovers the fraud I have perpetrated against her. I fear it more with every day that passes. I have been lucky so far, but we have not always lived in isolation and I dread that someone will recognise me."

"No one suspects it. You are safe, I tell you, and it will mean a great deal if you stay. Say you will, for Evangeline's sake if not for mine."

She smiled at him lovingly. "Very well, if it means so much to you, but only until the betrothal."

He looked troubled. "Evangeline will be sorely hurt when you do leave."

"Only for a short while, I promise you. She will be busy elsewhere, preparing for her wedding and setting up her own home. She will not fret for long."

"What will you tell her when the time comes?"

A shadow passed across her face. "I shall continue to be a coward, no doubt, and leave a note." She passed a hand across her brow. "I will think of something to tell her when the time comes, never fear, nor will anyone connect us. When you marry no one will expect Papa to attend, and perfectly understand why your sister cannot leave him."

"Does that mean you will never come to London for fear of recognition?"

Miranda felt desolate. "I believe it would be best. It wouldn't be necessary if I had but waited, and banishment for ever is the price I must pay for my folly."

"The price is too high! You have done no real wrong, Miranda. You did not want this masquerade; Dornford forced it on you."

She smiled sadly. "While that is true, I fear I did not think the matter out well enough. If Dornford hadn't come along, I should have been a burden and an embarrassment to you." Suddenly she jumped to her feet. "I must return now to Dornford House, before I am missed."

He hurried with her to the door. "How did you contrive to escape this morning?"

"I left before the others were up and I know Evangeline will be occupied for most of the morning having her hair dressed by that new man from France, Monsieur Duvalle. Nevertheless she will expect me to join her in her boudoir. Try to find a hackney carriage rather than a chair, it will be quicker."

He managed to hail one within a very few minutes and as he was about to hand her inside she turned and embraced him.

"Myles, I really couldn't wish for a sweeter sister even though I must of necessity never see her again. I am so glad for you both. I give you my blessing now in the event I cannot later."

With no further ado she climbed into the

carriage whilst her brother gave the jarvey his direction. As the hackney jerked into movement Miranda turned to wave to him and then sank back into the seat. Despite her relief that Myles's intentions towards Evangeline were after all genuine, she still could not prevent the tears from trickling down her cheeks, and as she fumbled in her pocket for a handkerchief she reflected rather sourly that weeping was becoming a fast established habit with her.

Chapter Eleven

The announcement of the coming marriage between Lady Evangeline Devilliars and Mr. Myles Templeton was made to coincide with a ball to be held at Dornford House. Evangeline, radiant in a gown of fuschia satin, was as always the centre of attention, but on this occasion she was surrounded by those who desired to wish her happy. The marquis also appeared well satisfied with his sister's choice. Dressed in his dark blue evening coat, the diamond pin sparkling on his cravat, he wandered amiably amongst his guests. No doubt, Miranda thought sourly, he was relishing the prospect of handing over responsibility for his sister's well-being to another in a short time. He would then be free to pursue his own life with even more dissipation than before. The thought pained her, for she was certain, basically, he could be as giving as his sister. Only the love of a woman was like to change him and Miranda doubted he would accept that.

It did her heart good, though, to see Evangeline so radiant, and she had to admit she had never seen Myles in such high spirits. It was an occasion to rejoice, but deep down inside her she was crying out in anguish. The time was drawing near for her to leave, and yet she dreaded to do so.

So real was her anguish she could eat no supper and caused Cornelius to retort, "Really, Miranda, you are quite unlike yourself of late. I would have thought this betrothal would have delighted you."

"So it has," she assured him. "I could not be happier. It's merely the heat and excitement of it all which has robbed me of my appetite."

Satisfied he leaned closer to her, saying in a coy voice, "Does Lady Evangeline's happiness not make you wish to share it, and not as a sister?"

His meaning was quite clear to her and she answered in some confusion, "Oh, indeed I do. Every woman wishes to find so congenial a match."

"Seeing Myles so happy makes me realise what I am missing." Then, lowering his voice he added urgently, "Miranda, we *must* talk. This masquerade has gone on long enough. We never see each other without there being a dozen others present also. You do know what I am trying to say, don't you?"

She glanced across the room and getting to her feet said in a breathless voice, "We cannot

possibly talk now, Cornelius. I believe Evangeline is beckoning to me. I must go to her."

In truth Evangeline was deep in conversation with Fanny Haygarth and as Miranda approached she shot her an unwelcoming look,
which, although it puzzled her, was sufficient
to cause her to leave the supper room instead
and seek a sanctuary elsewhere.

Lady Berriman, her hair towering above all
others, her elaborate gown liberally adorned
with diamonds, bore down on her unsuspecting
host who did not espy her until she was at his
side and therefore he had no chance to avoid
her.

"Lord Dornford, this is indeed a happy occasion for both families," she said using a tone
which implied a kinship and so irritated the
marquis, although he hid it well.

"It is gratifying to see my sister so well settled. It is," he added, a trifle maliciously, "to be
hoped that everyone may see their dependants
so well settled."

Lady Berriman's smile faded a little and she
sighed and glanced to where her own daughters stood in a huddle together by the dance
floor. "Oh, indeed." She raised her quizzing
glass and peered across to where Miranda was
laughingly in conversation with several young
people.

"Lady Evangeline's little friend, I note, is
still in residence. She is fortunate to have so

generous a host, for her stay has become rather a long one."

Unperturbed the marquis replied, "It was intended to be."

The woman's eyes narrowed. "She is something of a mystery, is she not?"

"Not to me, Lady Berriman."

"But one knows so little of her."

Her heavy musk perfume threatened to overcome him and he raised his own perfumed handkerchief in an effort to counteract the irritation. "From the point of view of general interest, there is little to know."

Where the most persistent gossip might have been forgiven for relinquishing the chase at this point, Lady Berriman pressed on, her obsequious manner hardening a trifle.

"I think it may have escaped your notice, Lord Dornford, but the chit has been seen rather often in the company of Mr. Osborne." The marquis fixed her with a steely glare and although she faltered a little she did continue, "Not that I would deem to criticise Lady Pendlebury as a chaperone, only one is bound to notice the attachment, and there has been no sign of any relatives that I can discover. . . ." She laughed in embarrassment. "I mean, well, to be plain, is it possible we may expect *another* announcement before long?"

He pondered carefully for what seemed to be a long moment. "I would say," he murmured at last, "that, yes, there is a possibility."

The woman straightened up, peering at Miranda unawares once more. "Well, I must own it is quite a remarkable thing. She is tolerably well-favoured, I admit, but a trifle *shabby*, wouldn't you say?"

"I am not and do not hope to be an arbiter of female fashion, Lady Berriman."

"Osborne is one of Lord Heldon's grandsons —from a younger son I do agree—but all the same I am persuaded Miss Crawley. . . ."

All signs of indulgence were gone from the marquis's manner now and Lady Berriman's voice died away in confusion as she became aware of it. In a cold voice which was famed for its cutting quality amongst those who displeased him, he said, "Lady Berriman, I made no mention of Mr. Osborne." Smiling stiffly he added, "Do excuse me, my lady, but I must propose a champagne toast before the dancing resumes."

She opened her mouth to make some answer but with unusual impoliteness he turned on his heel before she was able to speak.

Miranda listened politely to the stridently falsetto voice of Millicent Berriman who was singing "Where the bee sucks" to the assembled audience, and although few were actually enjoying the recital they certainly welcomed the rest from dancing.

Suddenly she realised that the marquis was gazing at her from across the room and she quickly averted her eyes from his. It was not the first time she had found herself the object of his intensive scrutiny that evening, which made her wonder if he suspected something was amiss with her. How long ago it seemed since their first encounter at the "Bell". Her cheeks still blushed at the memory of it, although she constantly strove to put it from her mind. But she could not, no more than she could forget that kiss which had so abruptly unhinged her reason, for it was only since that night her moods had been affected so disastrously.

Now she was so often prey to melancholy and self-denigration. That chance meeting at the "Bell" had changed the life of her brother too—for the better it was true—but more profoundly it had changed her own. Glancing across the room at the marquis again she knew why. Her life could never be happy again if she were to leave this house and forswear to see him again.

A hand on her arm made her start out of her unwelcome ruminations, and with a heart sinking even further she looked up to find Cornelius at her side. He was so fair of face and figure, and yet the sight of him no longer thrilled her heart.

"Miranda," he said in a low, urgent voice, "we can talk now in the hall whilst the Berriman chit gives what passes for a recital."

She was about to refuse, but then rose and followed him into the comparative quiet of the hall where several flunkies who had been lounging now jumped to attention.

Cornelius mopped his perspiring brow with his handkerchief. "Miranda, when is this foolishness to stop? You are Sir William Templeton's daughter. You cannot continue pretending you are a paid companion, prey to the condescension of those who are not your superiors."

"You are right. I intend to return home within the next few days. If anyone chooses to believe it is because I had set my heart on Myles, then so be it."

He looked relieved. "Once you are settled I shall take the first opportunity of calling on Sir William, to seek his permission to pay my addresses to you."

She looked away from him in distress. "I beg you do not. It will be to no avail."

"Miranda, have I not made myself plain? I wish to marry you. I was dazzled by Lady Evangeline for a while, but I soon came to my senses when I clapped eyes on you again."

Still averting her eyes she whispered, "This is painful for me to say, Cornelius, but I do not want to marry you."

"Miranda!" he cried in astonishment and then, lowering his voice, "Don't be missish with me. How can you expect me to believe that when you risked life and limb and your father's wrath to join me in London?"

"Yes, I know, and I did truly have a fondness

for you, only it was not deep enough and it is well I have discovered that now."

"My God," he said with a sneer, "females are the most damnable creatures. First Evangeline fluttering her eyelashes at me, and then you."

Distressed beyond belief she told him, "Cornelius, we are of the same age, you and I. It is wrong. You need someone younger and I someone older."

"Do you have someone in mind?"

Shrinking away from him she said in a harsh voice, "No!" They glared at each other for some few moments before she went on in a gentler way, "I did not mean to be a turncoat and I am sorry if you do truly care."

Without warning he caught hold of her. "I do care and the devil take me if I don't prove it to you!"

Despite her desperate struggle to free herself he did kiss her thoroughly and Miranda was furious, for there were servants about who were smirking at the spectacle.

"I will teach you to care for me again," he vowed. "You have only been dazzled by all you have seen and done since you came here. Don't you understand I can afford to keep you in just such style?"

"Mr. Osborne," said a silky voice, "I believe Miss Crawley wishes to return to the ballroom."

At last Cornelius freed her, turning angrily on his heel to face a laconic Lord Dornford.

"This is a private matter between Miss . . . Crawley and me."

"Not if she is unwilling, and from what I could see that is the case."

In truth, far from being relieved at the interruption, Miranda wanted to die. Her humiliation was far worse than that night at Vauxhall. This time he knew who she was, or at least thought he did which was much the same.

Cornelius's face grew red and for the first time Miranda realised he had been partaking of the wine quite freely all evening, which would account for his boldness although it did not lessen her own shame.

"Perhaps, my lord," he went on, "you will allow me to explain." He glanced at Miranda and then away again. "There are one or two matters which should be brought to your attention, and this is as good a time as any to do it."

She drew in a sharp breath but Lord Dornford remained resolute. "We must return to the ballroom, Mr. Osborne. After you."

"Lord Dornford, I insist on speaking with you right now."

The steely look came into his eyes again. "And I insist that you return to the ballroom immediately. If you have anything to say to me regarding Miss Crawley I shall be at home at noon tomorrow."

Miranda put her hand up to her lips to stifle a cry of dismay and flinging one last defiant look at her Cornelius hurried towards the front door, collected his hat and cane and stalked out of the house into the night.

The marquis put his hand out to her. "Are you recovered, Miss Crawley?" he asked in some amusement. When she nodded he took her arm. "It would appear Mr. Osborne is quite mad with love for you."

"It is more like he is bosky," she replied, discovering her voice again.

He drew her back towards the ballroom. "I wonder if he intends to declare himself when he returns at noon tomorrow. In the absence of any relatives, I must seem the appropriate person to approach on the matter."

Miranda looked up at him in alarm. "No!"

His face took on a look of surprise. "No? Well, what do you suppose he wishes to speak to me about?"

Near to fainting now she gasped, "I cannot imagine."

The musicians were playing a country dance and the gay atmosphere was suddenly alien to her. She longed to escape him, but he kept hold of her arm.

"If he does offer for you, do you wish to accept?"

"No!"

"Are you certain, Miss Crawley? Such an opportunity is not like to come again."

"I would not make him happy, Lord Dornford."

"I did believe you harboured a fondness for the boy."

"I did, and indeed still do, but not enough to become his wife." She looked up at him again and he said, "I bow to your wisdom in such matters. As far as I am concerned that is your decision and I will tell him of it if the need arises.

"You may be glad to know I have heard from my land steward at Dornford Place." She looked at him again, interest quickening now.

"How is Luke?"

"My steward informs me that he has settled down at last, after one or two initial problems."

"Oh?"

He smiled. "He threw a bag of flour at the cook and kicked her in the shins."

She tried desperately not to laugh. "The problem really is that he dislikes kitchen work, Lord Dornford."

"Almost as much as sweeping chimneys, it appears. He has been transferred to the stables now and shows a surprising aptitude in handling horses."

Miranda's face flushed once more, this time with pleasure. "I am so glad. It has been a great worry to me."

"And to me," he added dryly.

There was a pause, a discomforting one

whilst she waited for him to take his leave of her but he did not and she said, "Will you excuse me, Lord Dornford? I would like some lemonade."

"Allow me to procure some for you."

She began to protest, but he escorted her to the ante room and watched her as she sipped at it. Fortuitously he was obliged to leave her there in order to participate in a promised dance with one of his guests. The moment he had gone she put down the glass, jumped to her feet, and hurried back into the ballroom to ascertain that he was indeed dancing, before she sought out her brother. When she finally found him in one of the crowded ante rooms she was obliged to draw him away from a group of his cronies before she could speak freely.

"What's amiss?" he asked laughingly. "You look to be in quite a pucker."

"It's Cornelius! He's going to tell Lord Dornford about me!"

His smile faded. "The devil take him. Where is he? I shall deal with him. He's had a glass too much champagne. I'll warrant."

"He has already left, Myles, and promises to return at noon tomorrow. Lord Dornford has granted him an interview. I cannot remain here whilst he tells the marquis the entire story. You might catch up with him, but in all likelihood it will be too late. I don't want to leave you to face Lord Dornford's wrath and I shall leave a note exonerating you from blame, but I cannot remain to face him!"

Myles sighed deeply. "That is understandable. He will not look upon me so kindly, but that is of little consequence. What would you have me do?"

"I would like to leave as soon as I am able, the manner is of no consequence at all. I'd as lief walk to Sussex rather than remain here now."

He gazed down at her. "Evangeline will be desolate but I fear it is the only thing to do now. I will arrange for a post-chaise to call at dawn. Can you be ready for then?"

"Yes, oh yes, and I am grateful to you, dearest."

"Don't dare to thank me. You know I would do anything in my power for you."

She put her hand on his arm. "Myles, I'm so sorry to cause you this pain. Evangeline will forgive you, won't she?"

He smiled reassuringly. "She will think it the greatest lark when I explain fully. At least if the truth is known you will eventually be able to meet again."

"I could not face her."

"Oh, you know Evangeline. She will insist and she will also soothe Dornford's anger too."

"*He* will not forgive me."

"That at least will make no odds to you."

"Oh, it does, Myles, it does," she whispered. His eyes opened wide as he slowly comprehended her meaning. "Miranda! Oh, my dear. Dornford of all men. I am surprised at you. What are you to do about it?"

"Do not waste your pity on me. 'Tis no more than I deserve. I am in a fix of my own making. Now where is Evangeline? I fancy I haven't seen her for a while."

"Nor have I and I cannot think where she can have gone. I saw her dancing with that painted and powdered macaroni, Collingsby, but that was some time ago, before the musical recital. Will you go and look for her for me?"

"Of course I will, dearest."

She hurried away, visiting each ante room in turn, but no sign of Evangeline could be found. It was odd, for the girl loved to dance and was so rarely away from the ballroom whilst the music played. She began to be somewhat alarmed when a would-be partner for a minuet could not find her either.

After a while Miranda hurried up the stairs, extricating herself on several occasions from those who would stop her and wish to talk about Evangeline's betrothal and one or two others which were rumoured about to be announced. At last she reached the only place left to look—Evangeline's apartment—although Miranda regarded it unlikely the girl would be there. She knocked on the door and on receiving no reply was about to go away again when a sound from within arrested her. She paused and listened before quietly opening the door. To her amazement Evangeline was lying across the bed sobbing her heart out.

She hesitated no longer and flew across the room. "Oh, my dear, what is the trouble?" The girl did not stir; she just continued to sob. "Evangeline? Please talk to me. Tell me what's amiss with you. Are you ill? In pain?"

At last she did turn her tear-stained face towards Miranda. "Please leave me alone, Miranda. I do not care to talk to you."

"Why? Evangeline, this should be the happiest of nights for you. I cannot comprehend what has overset you. Dearest, confide in me, I beg of you."

The girl began to wipe her eyes with the handkerchief Miranda had given to her. "Yes, indeed this should be the happiest night of my life and would be if it were not for that cat, Fanny Haygarth, and *you.*"

Evangeline kept her eyes studiously averted. "Me?" Miranda stammered. "Why me? What have I done? Please tell me, Evangeline, for I cannot bear your distress."

The girl blew her nose. "You and your deceit have ruined my life. I shall never marry. Tomorrow I intend to retire to a nunnery for the remainder of my days."

At so dramatic a statement Miranda was tempted to laugh but her friend was too genuinely distraught. "My . . . deceit, you say."

Evangeline looked at her at last through eyes still brimming with tears. "Fanny could not wait to tell me. I have never seen anyone so well-pleased with herself. Last Friday morning she visited Pomeroy's Circulating Library in St. James's Street. . . ." Miranda's heart was full of foreboding. "Whilst she was waiting for her carriage to arrive she saw Myles come out of his lodgings and hail a hackney. She thought it odd to see him abroad in his dressing gown, and then she saw you come out and. . . ." she averted her eyes once more, ". . . embrace him as you left."

Miranda took a deep breath as Evangeline began to weep anew. "You said you did not love him. If only you'd admitted you did, I would have stood aside gladly. I would not have hurt *you* so, whatever the cost. Oh, I curse the day Dornford brought you home!"

She sank down on her knees by the bed, grasping Evangeline's hands tightly in her own. "Oh, please stop weeping, Evangeline, for I cannot bear it. I promise you there is nothing of that nature between Myles Templeton and myself. How could you think I would hurt you so, or even behave in so shameful a manner?"

"But you do not deny you were there at his lodgings."

"I was there, but not because we have an amorous liaison. There are matters which I cannot divulge even to you just now, but I assure you, you have nothing to fear. My reason for being in St. James's Street has nothing to do with you or Myles's feelings for you. He loves you to distraction."

Evangeline looked hopeful. "Truly?"

"Yes, truly. I have never seen a man so much in love. Will you trust me enough to believe in me?"

Slowly she nodded. "I did not wish to believe ill of you, Miranda, only I could not conceive of why you should be there. Next to Myles, James and Aunt Malzena, I love you best."

Miranda withdrew her hands and got to her feet. Her heart twisted within her breast at so touching a declaration which bitter-sweet as it was, would serve for all time as payment for her misdemeanour.

She was aware of Evangeline's continuing interest in her and as she laced and unlaced her fingers in agitation the girl said, "Can you not confide in me, Miranda? You know you can rely upon me to keep a secret whatever it may be."

In a choked voice Miranda answered, "Be assured all will soon be made clear to you. To-morrow, if you will only have the patience to wait, all will be known."

"Then I shall have to wait. Do you truly not love Myles?"

"Truly. In fact," she added with some difficulty, "I am in love with another."

The girl brightened up considerably at this news. "It is not the secret you imagine, Miranda, for I do believe I know who you mean."

She gave a broken laugh. "I doubt that," she murmured beneath her breath. No one will ever know apart from Myles.

Suddenly Evangeline jumped excitedly to her feet. "I have it! The answer has come to me at last!"

Miranda turned on her heel to face her wide-eyed. The girl's eyes sparkled brightly once more as she clasped her hands together in delight. "There is only one reason why you should visit him at his lodgings. There is kinship between you. Do not seek to deny it!"

"What . . . what makes you so certain?"

"I see it clearly now—the likeness. And I recall now once coming into your room before your hair was powdered. 'Tis the same unusual colour, which is now becoming so fashionable. Soon you will not need to powder at all, for it is about to become all the rage!"

Miranda was shaken to the very root of her being at this unexpected piece of astuteness. "You are very clever," she managed to murmur.

"And it is so good of you to keep the secret, to avoid the embarrassment of everyone knowing he has a poor relation forced to seek employment, but no one need know you are my paid companion and I am sure Myles would not really mind acknowledging the connection. Did he think it would matter to me?"

Miranda laughed shakily. "Dear Evangeline, please respect my wishes and keep the knowledge of our kinship to yourself. It is I, not Myles, who wishes it not to be known."

"The terrors of the inquisition would not drag it out of me."

Miranda gave her a quick kiss on the cheek before saying more briskly, "You must return to your guests before they realise you have gone."

It was then that Evangeline gasped in dismay, touching her face. "I cannot. I must look like a hag."

"Indeed you do not," Miranda laughed. She hurried to the dressing table and picked up the patch box and the haresfoot and rouge. "First a little rouge and then a few of these patches, and no one will know anything was ever amiss."

"And we shall return arm in arm to the ballroom to show that cat, Fanny Haygarth, her ruse has failed."

As Miranda began to fix the patches to Evangeline's cheeks she drew a sigh and her brow knitted into a frown. If dear, scatty, Evangeline had seen the likeness how long before others did so too? It was as well she would be gone for ever before the night was properly over.

Miranda surveyed the empty rooms of Dornford House and was glad it was the servants and not she who would have the task of clearing away the results of the night's revelry.

As the ormolu clock on the mantel chimed the hour she reflected she would not get to her bed that night. There would be time only for her to change into more modest travelling attire and to write explanatory notes to both Evangeline and the marquis before Myles would arrive in the hired post-chaise. At least her mode of arrival at the Templeton estate would be more dignified than that in which she left. That, she thought with a sigh, was a long time ago. The rash girl who left home so precipitously was no more. In her place was an older and wiser one.

A footstep in the doorway made her turn. "Not in bed yet, Miss Crawley?" asked the marquis.

He folded his arms and leaned against the doorpost, watching her. She forced a smile to her lips. "I was just about to retire. Evangeline has already gone up."

He remained in the doorway, looking at her and she was very much aware this might be her last sight of him, and her heart felt heavy with the knowledge.

"Only you and I remain downstairs now."

Only too well aware of it she moved towards the door, affecting a bright smile and yet never daring to look directly at him. "That is true and I shall go up immediately." He stepped aside to allow her past and she murmured, "Good night, Lord Dornford."

She had just reached the hall when he said,

"Your god-mother, Lady Berriman, is well pleased at your brother's betrothal."

She turned on her heel, unable to believe her ears. "My. . . .? Lord Dornford, what did you say?"

His face was devoid of any expression which added to her bewilderment. "You heard, Miss Templeton, or may I call you Lenore?"

She stiffened at that. "No one has ever called me Lenore. I have always been known as Miranda, which is my second given name. You haven't . . . known *all* the time, have you?"

He smiled. "No. I didn't know who you were until a few weeks ago, but I've always known you were not who you claimed to be at the inn."

Bewildered she came further into the room and said, "But you believed what I told you. You did!"

He sat down on a sofa and stretched his legs out before him. "What makes you think I am such a fool to believe so obvious a farrago of lies? The tale was transparently false even if I had not chanced to read a portion of a novel called . . . now let me see . . . ah yes, I recall it—*The Tribulations of Magdelain*. I was obliged to wait some considerable time in a certain lady's boudoir and I grew bored enough to pick up the book. The plot, you obviously recall, exactly mirrors the tale of iniquity you related to me, substituting different names for the characters, of course. With her preoccupation for novels I only wonder Evangeline had not read it too."

Miranda sank down on the edge of the sofa. "If that were not enough to damn you, I had only just left the home of one Squire Fazackerly, an elderly bachelor who wished to sell me his land."

She buried her head in her hands. "How can I ask your forgiveness, Lord Dornford?"

"I assure you it's unnecessary. You will recall I forced you into the position whereby you had no choice but to tell me a Banbury Tale. Had you confessed the truth you were well aware I would have returned you home forthwith. As it is the best I could do was to appear to accept the tale and bring you here where I was sure you would be safe and out of mischief until I could discover what you were really up to.

"It seemed clear you had a good reason to be coming to London—your desperate measures to do so convinced me of that—and it was obvious you must know someone already residing here. Your secrecy made me curious. My only fear of late has been that mayhap your father would appear like an avenging angel, or at the very least a Runner."

"Papa believes me to be safely in Cheltenham with an old school friend and her widowed mother." Without looking at him she was aware he was smiling, enjoying his revenge on her. "When did you discover who I was?" she asked although it was becoming increasingly difficult for her to speak at all.

"I began to note an affinity between you and Templeton. At first I believed you had run away to join your lover, but then one day whilst we were riding in the park you turned to each other and laughed. It was like seeing a mirror image. When Osborne began to pay his attentions to you the matter became even clearer to me. He was the lover you had run away to join. After these facts were established the rest was easy to confirm by a few simple enquiries.

"Myles Templeton did indeed have a spirited sister, attendant on an eccentric father, with no chance of a Season. With my knowledge of your nature, it was all very clear."

"You knew weeks ago," she said, turning to him angrily. "And I have suffered all manner of agonies of guilt!"

He threw back his head and laughed, spreading his arms out along the back of the sofa. "It is no more than you deserve, but it is good to see that spirit in you again."

"Be content, my lord, your revenge is better than you know." She got to her feet. "I will be gone from here before you are down to breakfast."

He eyed her in amusement. "You are not transforming yourself into a boy again, are you?"

She stiffened. "Certainly not. Myles is coming with a post-chaise."

"You relieve me, but what makes you think, after all these weeks, gammoning me in my own home, I would allow you to go so easily?"

Her eyes sparkled with anger once more. "What would you have to gain by detaining me further?"

He regarded her from beneath half-closed lids. "Mayhap a wife." Miranda gazed at him, speechless now and unconsciously twisting her hands before her. "Pray, be merciful, my angel, put me out of my misery by saying yes or no."

Her hands flew to her cheeks which now flamed red. "It is now you who are gammoning *me*."

He sat up, alert now. "No, Miranda, let us be finished with jest now. I love you although I fear that life with you will be no restful matter."

Fearing that her legs would no longer support her she sank down onto the edge of the sofa once more. "Oh, my goodness," she breathed. "I cannot believe this."

He was close by her side a moment later, drawing her unprotesting in his arms. He gazed into her face, taking in every aspect of it and then he cupped it in his hands kissing her gently. His kisses affected her as much as on the last time he embraced her, and she could no more resist than on that occasion.

When he released her at last he said softly,

"You see, you have proved something beyond a doubt."

"And that is?" she asked breathlessly.

"I have a heart and it belongs to you."

She clung to him tightly for a long time before emerging to ask in sudden alarm, "That night at Vauxhall. . . .?"

"Oh yes, I remember it." She looked at him, unable to frame her question and presently he said, "You may be sure I knew whom I kissed. You'd tempted me for too long and when I realised it *was* you and you had no other business alone on that path save for a rendezvous with Osborne, I could not resist teasing you. I was mad with jealousy—an unfamiliar emotion for me—and determined to have my revenge for the havoc you were playing with my feelings."

"You have been very hard on me."

"If that is so I apologise. In the future life will be much easier for you in every way. All that remains is for me to approach your father in the proper manner and I envisage no obstacle there."

"He will agree to anything in an effort to return to his writing."

"Especially, I fancy, when I offer him the unrivalled facilities of the library at Dornford Place." He smiled down at her. "For that he would give you into the hands of a slaver."

She laughed and as he kissed her again she relaxed against him, wishing this enchanted evening might now never end. Then suddenly she drew away, saying in great distress, "Oh, I cannot marry you. I cannot."

He sat up straight but he was still very close to her and she longed to throw herself into his arms again. "Do you think me too old?"

"Oh no. Not at all, and I love you dearly."

"Then there is another with prior claim to your affections?"

She shook her head. "Not mine." She looked at him. "Simply, I cannot share *you* with another. I know it is quite commonplace for wives to do so, but to be plain I would find it intolerable and our life together would suffer for it."

Her head drooped and he put one finger beneath her chin to raise it so he could look into her eyes once more.

"Let me tell you something; Lady Bascombe, to whom you refer, has been a close friend of mine for more than ten years. Would that she could remain so for many more years, but that cannot be. She is mortally ill, Miranda, although mercifully she is not aware of it."

Miranda was truly shocked. "How can this be?"

"Every physician who has examined her gives the same opinion."

Her eyes filled with tears. "How terrible. She is still young and beautiful."

"It is a very heavy burden to bear. Those of

us who are close to her are striving to ensure her last weeks are as happy as possible. She was so happy to meet you, Miranda. Even though I remain fond of her she has known for a long, long time she no longer holds my heart."

Tears sparkled on her eyelashes. "She knows all about me, doesn't she? She knew that I was no servant the day we visited her."

"She is one of the few in whom I can confidently confide. I hope you are not angry."

"How can I be?"

"I trust you will treat this information as a confidence." She nodded and he went on in a lighter vein, "As to the future, I believe I shall be well occupied keeping you out of mischief. There will be little time for others."

"I will make sure of it," she assured him. "But answer me one more question and I will bury my jealousies for ever."

"Ask it."

She put her hand up to the scar on his cheek. "Who was the lady over whom you duelled?"

He stared at her in astonishment and then threw back his head and laughed. She waited until his laughter had abated a little before saying, "Do you think me ridiculous for wishing to know?"

He looked at her lovingly. "I admit I did once fight a duel in my wild youth, but it was over a suspect hand of cards and we both missed any mark. This," he added, laughing again as he touched the scar, "is the result of my first attempts at riding. I fell off the pony and cracked my head on a stone. Not quite such a romantic tale I'm afraid!"

Miranda laughed too. "I'm delighted to hear it. I promise not to plague you again with such questions."

"I'm delighted that you concede defeat to me without my mentioning my trump card."

She affected to look outraged. " 'Tis not defeat, but victory for me, but pray don't let me deprive you of producing your trump card."

"Luke, of course. You do wish to see him again."

She smiled broadly. "I admit it will be good to see him growing up, gaining in strength with each passing day."

"I could not face the prospect without you," he murmured dryly.

He kissed her again and they remained in a tight embrace until the clock once more struck the hour. Almost immediately the chimes died away the sound of a carriage could be heard approaching the house.

"That must be Myles!" she gasped.

The marquis squeezed her hand and got to his feet. "There seems no point in allowing the poor fellow to remain out there in the cold. I'll go and admit him. I have already promised him some of my best claret and this is as good a time as any to break open a bottle, don't you think?"

She laughed, imagining Myles waiting apprehensively outside. "Yes, do invite him in. We can all have breakfast together and discuss our respective wedding plans!"

FREE
Fawcett Books Listing

There is Romance, Mystery, Suspense, and Adventure waiting for you inside the Fawcett Books Order Form. And it's yours to browse through and use to get all the books you've been wanting . . . but possibly couldn't find in your bookstore.

This easy-to-use order form is divided into categories and contains over 1500 titles by your favorite authors.

So don't delay—take advantage of this special opportunity to increase your reading pleasure.

Just send us your name and address and 35¢ (to help defray postage and handling costs).

FAWCETT BOOKS GROUP
P.O. Box C730, 524 Myrtle Ave., Pratt Station, Brooklyn, N.Y. 11205

Name _____
(please print)

Address _____
City _____ State _____ Zip _____

Do you know someone who enjoys books? Just give us their names and addresses and we'll send them an order form too!

Name _____
Address _____
City _____ State _____ Zip _____

Name _____
Address _____
City _____ State _____ Zip _____